THE BOY OF ASHES

The Boy of Ashes

Luke Huard

For all who have dreamed

"They were careless people, Tom and Daisy—they smashed up things and creatures and then retreated back into their money or their vast carelessness, or whatever it was that kept them together, and let other people clean up the mess they had made"

—The Great Gatsby

Contents

Prologue vii

Part One 1
  1 Chapter 1 2
  2 Chapter 2 16
  3 Chapter 3 25
  4 Chapter 4 30
  5 Chapter 5 51
  6 Chapter 6 62

Part Two 77
  7 Chapter 7 78
  8 Chapter 8 83
  9 Chapter 9 95
  10 Chapter 10 108

Part Three 112
  11 Chapter 11 113
  12 Chapter 12 118

| 13 | Chapter 13 | 122 |
| 14 | Chapter 14 | 132 |

Prologue

"Why are you always so mad at the world, Martin? What did anyone ever do to you?"

"I'm not mad at the world, but sometimes I'm just…bitter, that's all—you wouldn't understand. There's nothing wrong with that. You are far from the only person who doesn't understand what I've been through. Regardless, I still love you—I promise. Remember, I'm not like those men out on East and West Egg that used to chase you. I know you miss those parties. However, I'm of a new—of a new breed of businessmen. We don't do parties."

"I know, but you never talk about your family—or how we have all of this money. You always tell me, 'Otto would be proud,' as if I'm somehow supposed to know what that means. Who even is Otto? Why do we have to stay here in this awful place if we're doing so well? Martin, we're getting married next week, and I feel like I barely know you."

"Fine. I suppose I'll tell you what you can handle, but that's it—nothing more. You're too… sensitive for most of the details. After I tell you, we'll *never* talk about it again. Deal?"

"Yes, but tell me the truth, Martin—the *real* truth."

Part One

1

Chapter 1

A cloud of ash attacked my nostrils as I undid the six deadbolts that lined the wooden frame of Otto's front door. The night before, he had checked each lock twice before heading off to bed.

That hot summer morning, the sun dangled above the Valley of Ashes like an orange waiting to be picked by the impatient farmer. A band of golden rays stabbed the mountains of ash, casting long shadows on the endless industrial sprawl below. In the shadows, vice avoided the sun's revealing glare as it consumed the tri-state area.

Mischief ran rampant those days, but I, lacking the necessary maturity to detect the finer nuances of life, was too naive ever to notice. Even if I had somehow noticed, there wasn't much for me to do about it—not then, at least.

It was 1922, but, more importantly, it was the warmest day of that year's sweltering summer. In our tiny industrial sliver of New York City, we envied the lavish lifestyles many had grown accustomed to in that decade.

By the end of most days, the men of the Valley of Ashes trudged home, drenched in sweat, ready to change into a dry set of clothes before indulging in a much-needed post-work meal. The night, despite its chilling allure, wasn't a refuge from the heat either. Sadly, there was no escaping the sun's wrath.

Like a fool, I decided to skip breakfast that morning. In the past, Donna, our young, unmarried neighbor, used to drop off a freshly baked pie at breakfast time for Otto and me to enjoy. On a lucky day, she used to drop off a blueberry pie, which was by far my favorite of her pies, after pecan and apple, of course. My nostrils fluttered as I took several breaths, and with every sniff, a mixture of ash and apples entered my nose—no blueberry pie for me.

Long ago, Donna had stopped bringing them over when she found out Otto had been peeking through her window, admiring…the *view*.

I remember that awful day when she pounded, with both of her fists, on the front door after he had committed *the deed*.

With each knock, the door rattled, almost falling off the hinges into the hallway. I thought it was an earthquake, but it was just the strength of a violated woman—that's all.

When I finally answered the door, Donna stood there with her arms crossed and her eyes evil, ready to kill whom she sought. She demanded to speak to Otto, but he had failed to appear in the doorway next to me.

Instead, Otto peered into the hallway, hiding the majority of his figure behind the wall, as Donna unleashed a flood of curses and unrepeatable epithets. With each word, her spit rained down on me.

After she slammed the door in my face, I turned to a still-hidden Otto and waited for him to provide me with a proper explanation, but he simply brushed it off with a joke.

How could I ignore such a lovely sight when I am always haunted by these hideous heaps of ash?

* * *

I attempted to tame my messy blonde hair but decided it was not worth my time and let it fall naturally instead. It gently bounced with each step I took.

When I went to close the front door behind me, it refused to close shut. I muttered a series of expletives under my breath as I adjusted my stance, grabbed the doorknob, and tugged.

Nothing.

After many years of use and abuse, the door frame, wildly warped from its original rectangular shape, refused to give in to my attempt to manhandle it.

The previous spring, Otto had dragged out his toolbox and tried to fix it, but it was useless—he was clueless when it came to repairing things that couldn't be fixed with the simple swing of a hammer or shovel. I suppose, looking back, I could have tried fixing it, too, but I never did.

I wiped my sweaty palms on my overalls and grabbed hold of the doorknob with both of my hands. The floorboards of the porch flexed beneath me as I dug in. I took a deep breath and pulled.

Still, nothing. The door refused to budge like a stubborn loose tooth.

A strong gust of wind blew the door ajar, almost pushing me down into the dirt. Growing impatient, I settled for leaving it cracked open about an inch.

Strong winds swept across the Valley day and night and often carried loose ash through open windows, holes in the roof, and, of course, front doors that had been left ajar. Like a professional army, the ash scouted for weak points to infiltrate and conquer, smothering all it embraced. I looked at the door once more, worried Otto would notice, but I ultimately capitulated, hoping he wouldn't think anything of it.

A few yards away from the porch, Otto sat swaying in his favorite beat-up rocking chair he had rescued from a trash heap destined for the dump. The chair's oak wood, stained a grayish-black like a piece of coal, lacked any hint of its original pasty white.

Otto, lightly dressed due to the sweltering heat, sipped his coffee, smoked his cigar, and read his newspaper before heading off to work. His rolls of fat hugged the rocking chair's arms, and his tiny legs dangled several inches off the ground.

Despite his grotesque figure, Otto held enough wisdom and knowledge to fill all the shelves of even the largest of the world's libraries. However, he appeared oblivious to the battle I had just lost to the front door, only a few yards away from his throne.

A cloud of smoke escaped as he temporarily withdrew the cigar from his mouth. His eyes scanned his newspaper like a mouse searching for a scrap of cheese. The newspaper, covered in German from top to bottom, prevented me from reading over his shoulder. To me, German looked like a secret code, but to him, it was the first language he had ever learned.

I suppose after the War ended, publishers lacked a supply of positive news to print about Germany and its people. Some days, Otto cried while reading his paper. It wasn't a violent cry, but the occasional tear leaked from the corner of his eyes, leaving stains that dotted the paper like a field of artillery craters.

On other days, he looked at the newspaper without any emotion as he concentrated on the stories he read. However, most days, he just looked irritated, as if every article reached out and stabbed his eyeballs before retreating to the safety of the paper.

"Martin, what did I tell you just last week about sleeping in late?" Otto grumbled as he looked up from his newspaper with critical eyes, still bloodshot from his night of heavy drinking.

I didn't have a good answer to his question, but I knew if I waited long enough, he would hit me with another question instead.

"Did you at least sleep well?" he asked with a slight smirk that was partially concealed by his bushy mustache.

Otto twirled his cigar through the air as a steady stream of smoke escaped, tickling his face. He paused and held the cigar in front of him as he waited for my answer; his eyebrows rose in anticipation as my silence persisted.

Otto was always willing to change a question once but never twice—he was stubborn like that. If you couldn't answer his second question, you were asking for trouble.

"I—I forgot to shut my window before getting into bed, and the rain was terribly loud last night. It kept me tossing and turning for most of the night. I didn't realize that it was open until I got up this morning," I said sheepishly, hoping Otto would find my answer satisfactory.

"Are you a moron?" Otto asked as he shook his round, hairless head and chuckled to himself.

He asked me that question rhetorically whenever he felt the need to reassert his dominance over me, reminding me that I was a guest in his house. He was the King, and I was a mere jester.

Otto had the unfortunate habit of indulging in the works of Henry Goddard. A copy of Goddard's book, *A Rise of the Colored Nations*, sat on his nightstand, filled with all sorts of twisted ideas of how he thought the world worked. Wealthy and poor men alike gravitated toward the hateful messages. I never took hold of them and slightly resented Otto for his unfortunate selection of a worldview.

Despite all of his flaws, Otto loved me like a son and had stepped up when no one else cared about me.

I trusted Otto to keep me safe, but beyond that, I didn't know him from a hole in the wall. He had worked with my father at the ash company when the mountains were still small piles. They were close friends all the way up until his death, bonding over the conservative line they held in the ever-changing world around them. Despite his abrasive personality, Otto took me in after I was orphaned. He let me sleep in a spare bedroom—which had been a closet his two daughters once shared.

Most of the time, Otto meant well but failed to follow through on his good intentions, leaving me utterly disappointed.

He enjoyed calling everyone a moron after they committed the slightest infraction. It was just something he did, and I quickly became accustomed to his habit. I had to learn to put up with him; otherwise, I'd be back living in the orphanage.

After finishing his morning newspaper, Otto took his lighter, held it to the corner of the paper, and watched it burn. A tiny pile of ashes formed on his lap.

A film of perspiration covered his forehead, and sweat stains began to form on the seams of his shirt. In an hour or two, he would be completely drenched from head to toe.

Looking out across the Valley, Otto assessed the piles of ash that sprung up like a mountain range, reaching high into the sky towards nothing but open air. Their virgin peaks were free from adventurous climbers—no one cared to climb something so sad. A flock of birds flew high over them, greeting us with their flapping wings while avoiding the putrid air below them.

"Must be flying South early, no?" Otto said with a slight smile, trying to be cordial with me for a change.

I nodded—some of his questions were best answered with only a slight nod of the head instead of a long-winded speech.

He rubbed his scruffy face, running his fingers over the cigarette-sized scar that crossed his cheek. I had asked him once how he got it.

"From when I was in the army over in Germany—before the war, of course," he had told me, but I doubted the accuracy of his explanation.

Otto rarely shaved, making him look straight out of the wanted posters published in the evening papers. Looking back now, perhaps I *had* seen him in the evening papers...

A few hundred yards in front of our porch, a string of train cars rattled along the tracks that bisected the Valley of Ashes. As they traveled, the train's wheels screamed like a baby calling out for their mother and father. I winced; I never entirely became numb to the train's cry; it often woke me up in the middle of the night, preventing me from sleeping soundly.

Beyond the set of tracks, clusters of automobiles traveled along the boulevard, sometimes passing through the Valley on roads littered with trash, ash, and discarded dreams. Most people had no desire to stay for long—unless they needed to stop for gas or visit a friend. Those who stayed risked getting their fancy shirts and summer dresses permanently stained with ash—and no one wanted that, of course.

Most days, Otto stayed in the Valley, unloading ash as it arrived from the City in carts and trucks driven by poor immigrants like himself. However, some days, he ventured into the City for his second job.

Every year, the mountains of ash grew higher, reaching up toward the clouds and blocking more and more sunlight from stroking the Valley with its restorative touch. Regardless, the sun fought to illuminate and infiltrate the Valley the best that it could.

Using all of his strength to push himself up, Otto rose from his rocking chair, waving his arms as if he were a tour guide pointing out the wonders of an unusual land to captivated tourists. He grinned as he admired the mountains built over the past couple of decades—but I knew deep down he would have done anything to bring about their demise.

"The company's starting a new ash dump tomorrow. One day, it might become the tallest pile we have in this hellhole. We'll be the envy of all of the other ash dumps, no?" Otto asked with a sarcastic chuckle, throwing his head back as he shook his head and smiled at the rising sun. Beads of sweat rolled down his neck.

I gave him a smirk and a nod of the head. I wasn't entirely sure where he was going with this.

No matter where you stood in the Valley, the mountains of ash were always in view. They stood like a row of shark's teeth, waiting patiently to shred apart the flesh of anyone who ventured too close.

When it rained, a noxious soup of ash and dirt formed in puddles throughout the Valley. One cup and you would have been able to escape the Valley of Ashes for good—that's what Otto used to tell me.

Otto turned to me and mockingly boasted, "People out in East Egg and West Egg think they have nice views? Bah! We have the best views right here in the Valley of Ashes. People would *kill* to have the views we have here. Wouldn't they, Martin?"

Otto let out a laugh as he enjoyed his joke; I simply nodded in agreement.

Otto *always* knew best—and he never missed an opportunity to indicate his superiority over you. However, this time, he made a good point; nobody liked living in the Valley of Ashes. Beyond the poor aesthetics, if you weren't used to it, the ash stabbed at your lungs with every breath, causing them to fail when you needed them the most.

You see, back then, the City relied on burning coal, but that left them with ash. At some point, the City had figured out it wasn't ideal to leave ash sitting outside every business and residence for innocent pedestrians to inhale as they walked by.

Their solution to this problem was great for the City—but not so great for us living in the Valley. Long ago, they began collecting the City's discarded ash in wagons and trucks. They hauled it away and carelessly dumped it down where the Flushing River meets the shore. As the piles of ashes grew into tall mountains, the Valley of Ashes was born.

We were the choke point between the City and Long Island. Almost all motor and train traffic squeezed their way through the Valley as they commuted between the City and their homes. They only had to deal with it on their daily commutes; we had to eat, sleep, and breathe it every single day.

Sure, I suppose we could have packed our bags and gone elsewhere, but without us, the whole City would have suffocated in less than a week.

Otto plopped back down in his chair and took a drag of his cigar.

"Are you working today, Martin?"

"Actually, I planned on taking a trip down to Wallabout Market to buy a crate of oranges and bring them back here," I stammered as I revealed to Otto my closely guarded plans for the first time.

"What for?" Otto inquired; his eyes expanded as he pre-emptively struck down my dream.

"You must have heard that they're shutting down the bridge over the river again."

"Yes. Of course, I've heard about it, Martin. I've heard *all* about it." Otto slapped his leg. "I've had multiple people complain to me about it just this morning alone. What does it have to do with this little scheme of yours?"

"Well, I thought I'd sell oranges to the drivers as they passed through on the detour."

Otto chuckled and took a sip from his mug. Without a cover, the coffee has become infused with a slight bit of ash. He let out a sigh as he grinned at me—but it was not a smile of approval.

"They'll all be covered with ash in an hour or so. No one will want to buy an ash-covered orange from a boy like you."

"I'll get a rag, and I'll wash them. I have it all planned out. I'm just chasing my dream."

"Dream? What dream?"

I paused and thought for a moment.

"My American Dream. The one my parents never got to finish."

"The American Dream is dead, just like your—" Otto cut himself off as he released a puff of smoke from his mouth.

He let out a bellowing laugh, tinged with an air of sophistication. Then, all joy quickly drained from his face after he realized the gravity of what he had just declared.

He continued with a slightly calmer tone, "Martin, if you were smart, you'd come to work for the ash company like the rest of us here in the Valley and be a man instead of chasing some childish dream. You want to make it out of here one day, right?" He shook his head. "Maybe you really are a—"

The screech of a passing train cut Otto off before he could deliver his final blow. Sparks spewed out from underneath it as it raced off towards the City.

From their carriages, the passengers looked down at us as if we were animals trapped in a city-sized zoo. A few young children poked their heads out from beneath their mother's arms to catch a glimpse of the bleak landscape and monkeys below. Their fathers, dressed in stiff suits, grimaced at the dismal landscape before them.

"Bah," Otto scoffed as the train bounced along the steel tracks. If it weren't for the children watching, he would have given them the finger.

Otto leaned forward and handed me a cup of coffee he had made fresh in the kitchen. Like most things in the Valley, it tasted like a campfire mixed with day-old rainwater. I held the cup with both of my hands but refused to drink any of it. In addition to the awful smell it gave off, it was too hot outside to be drinking coffee.

A permanent coating of ash lined my throat, and whenever I drank Otto's coffee, a nauseating mix of ash and black coffee grounds blended in my stomach, leaving me queasy for the rest of the day. Most days, I vomited at least once after eating or drinking anything prepared in the Valley.

Oh, and the air—you could never escape the unbearable air. Smog from the looming smokestacks settled in the low-lying Valley. Suddenly, it tickled the inside of my nose, and I let out a bellowing sneeze.

"Gesundheit," Otto said as he downed the last of his coffee, setting the empty mug down beside his rocking chair.

I sneezed a lot—more than the average person. However, I wasn't the average person. The average person didn't have to tolerate the air I had to breathe. Besides the constant presence of ash, there was plenty of dust, mold, and cobwebs scattered throughout the Valley. Otto didn't clean the house anymore; he was far too busy working his two jobs.

Otherwise, for the most part, my body had adjusted to living in the Valley. One of those fancy doctors in the City could have split me open and extracted a few pounds of ash from my body to make me better, but we didn't have any of them out here in the Valley.

If you wanted to see a doctor, you had to go deep into the City and pay more money than most people made in a year. Ash flowed through my blood, my heart, and my mind—I was the boy of ashes, half-corrupted but still hopeful for an ash-free future. One day, I planned to escape the Valley of Ashes and never return.

After the last train car passed, Otto turned to me, waving his hand as if it absolved him of all liability, and said, "You do whatever you want today, Martin. You're old enough to find out how this world really works. It's not as nice as you think it is."

I cocked my head sideways, but Otto didn't seem to notice my confusion. He only shook his head and chuckled to himself. Looking back, he was right.

Chapter 2

Otto and I watched as a few men struggled to push a stubborn wagon out of the mud. Half-smoked cigarettes hung from the corners of their mouths; the falling ashes formed tiny piles at their feet. The early morning heat didn't help their cause either. From this one small chore, they were already drenched in sweat; their white shirts were stained a dark gray, and their faces were red like slices of tomatoes.

I strained my ears, catching their muffled words as they yelled at each other:

"Three, two, one—push!" one of the men shouted as they all threw themselves against the back of the wagon.

After a brief moment of struggle, one of the other men backed off from the cart and complained, "You were hardly pushing. Why was I doing all the work? You have to push like you mean it! Otherwise, we aren't going anywhere."

His potbellied partner pointed his finger and insisted, "I am pushing. You're the one that isn't pushing, you lazy bum.

You're the one that got us stuck here in the first place. The sun isn't even up all the way, and you've already wrecked our day."

Otto shook his head as the men launched into a shoving match, hurling nasty insults at each other. For a moment, Otto looked tempted to get up and intervene. However, eventually, the men dragged each other down into the mud and rolled around like a couple of pigs. I couldn't help but laugh; Otto chuckled, too.

"On days like this, I wish I was back in Germany where I belong," Otto said with a slight frown, followed by a few puffs of his cigar.

A couple of decades before the turn of the century, Otto and his siblings had packed up what little they owned, boarded one of those gigantic passenger ships, and arrived at Ellis Island. Otto's parents stayed back in Germany so they could tend to the family farm while their children took a shot at the American Dream halfway across the world.

While most of his siblings continued their journey out west, Otto decided to settle down in New York City, specifically in the heart of the Valley of Ashes.

"Why don't you go and join your brothers and sisters out in Cleveland?" I asked.

Otto took a deep breath and said, "It's not that easy. Also, I'm looking out for you now, and despite the number of times I complain about it, the Valley does me great good. I shouldn't complain as much as I do. I shouldn't, but I do. I can't help myself."

"Wouldn't you be happier out there living with your family?"

Otto shrugged.

"No true way of knowing for sure. So, why go through the trouble just to stay miserable? It's not New York or the Valley of Ashes I hate. I hate America, Martin."

I know he didn't mean the people or the politics like some of the true anarchists did; he just hated living somewhere that wasn't Germany. Every night, he told me a story over dinner from when he lived in Germany, much happier than he was now. He admitted the United States had a lot more opportunities than Germany had ever had for him, but he still longed for his fatherland. It was a love-hate relationship, no doubt.

"They should have deported me during the War. I tried so hard to get them to. I told all of my neighbors that I was an anarchist and that I smuggled weapons, explosives—you name it, but nothing! They left me here to rot in the Valley. Bah!"

"How's Myrtle doing?" I asked, changing the subject away from his homesickness.

"Myrtle is the only daughter who still talks to me. Catherine's off in the City doing God knows what, and the only things I hear about her come through Myrtle."

"So, Myrtle's doing fine at least?"

"She's alright. She's still living with that sad excuse for a man, George Wilson. Oh, boy, what a moron! I went to see that tiny room she lives in with that fool—the one crammed above the garage. I expect so much more for my daughters—I really do, Martin. It's very embarrassing for her to live like that. Very embarrassing for a father to see his daughters live like that."

He spoke with such a conviction that his daughters deserved the world—as if they deserved to be married not to a greasy auto repairman but to some wealthy socialite on Long Island. Perhaps Otto was no better than any other father, or maybe he was delusional.

"Yeah…I've been in his auto shop before. He's an—odd man," I said.

"Odd? Just *odd*? The man's paranoid about everything and anything. He thinks the world is going to end every Friday night. He thinks I'm always up to no good around here. I'm just an old man. He's full-blown crazy, no?"

I shrugged and said nothing, unsure at that point what to say to appease Otto. One slip of the wrong word, and he'd tear you to shreds.

Otto continued, "I guess she enjoys the freedom from me, that's all. I offered to take her back in multiple times, but she refused. Stubborn girl—she takes after her father." Otto took a drag of his cigar. "I wasn't even that hard on the girls while they were growing up. I gave them everything and anything they wanted—spoiled little brats. I can't believe that I had considered leaving all of this for them," Otto said as he waved the palms of his hands around in the seemingly empty air. "Well, I have to leave now. Two jobs aren't going to work themselves. I'll see you later tonight, Martin."

Otto chucked aside the remnants of his cigar and walked off into the Valley.

I bolted back into the house and climbed the stairs in a hurry. Tucked in a tattered shoe box underneath my bed, I stored all of the loose change that I had found strewn around the Valley.

From my room, I had a view of the entirety of the Valley: the buildings, the people, and all of the mountains of ash. I felt like God, looking down on the automobile-infested streets below. I lacked any power to control what I saw, but my heart ached nonetheless. Power quickly corrupts; give a man an ounce of it, and he can cook a feast fit for an army.

Miles away, sunlight glistened off of the City's many skyscraping buildings. The ground shook as more trains slithered through the Valley like garden snakes. Slowly, they all made their way into the City. Cars outpaced the trains as they cruised steadily down the boulevard.

The occasional driver took a detour through the heart of the Valley of Ashes, educating their passengers on how the other half lived. Any smiles they once wore evaporated, and with their shrewd eyes, they judged us for how we lived. Their perfectly polished faces, stained ever so slightly from their trip through the Valley of Ashes, returned to normal once they realized our reality was just their temporary inconvenience.

Below my window, Joseph, the oldest and crabbiest of the Valley dwellers, solemnly pulled his cart of scrap metal, waddling like a duck with a broken leg. He stopped and dropped his cart below my window.

"Hi, Martin," he groaned up to me before letting out a slow sigh.

"Joseph? Is that you? Getting an early start today?"

Joseph insisted on everyone calling him by his first name despite being older than the wheel. His brothers lived out in Ohio; they owned a large farm that raked in immense profit. A few years back, they had dumped him off in the Valley after he accused one of them of running a bootlegging operation out of the family barn.

"Unfortunately, yes," he sighed, wiping a film of sweat from his forehead. "I have no choice. The boss said he needs me to work extra this week and the week after that, too. It seems we've had a surprise increase in business."

"That's nice. I'm sure that you're happy to—"

"No, it's not."

"What?"

"It's not nice. I don't want to work an extra twenty hours. I already work a fifty-hour week," Joseph mumbled with a frown.

He continued, "Sometimes I wonder why we all even bother getting up in the morning. What are we all even doing here? The day we die, they'll just grind us up or bury our bodies, lumping us in with the rest of the lot."

"That's awfully pessimistic. Don't you think?"

"No—No, I'm not a pessimist. I just don't get why everyone gets all worked up over things when, in the end, nothing really matters. When all of this is over—when we die—none of what we accomplished, hoped or dreamed will even be relevant anymore. Those petty arguments we fought will all be for nothing. Those we loved and lost have no bearing. You didn't make enough money for your employer to buy a new mansion? Who cares? It's all for nothing anyway."

"I suppose, but—are you okay, Joseph? You're awfully negative today."

"You know, Martin, the Devil runs large; he has his wicked fingers wrapped around every last thing in this Valley and—never mind. I'm fine. Thank you for asking; most people ignore me, but not you, boy—you always notice me. I might not be happy, but at least I'm fine. If I could die in exchange for the eternal happiness of others, I would."

"A little extreme, don't you think?"

"Perhaps, but I truly mean it—wouldn't it be great if it was that easy? I'd do it in a heartbeat. Wouldn't you?"

I wasn't prepared to have such a philosophical conversation that early in the morning, especially with someone like Joseph.

"I don't think so. To tell you the truth, I don't think it's even possible."

"To die?" Joseph asked with glossy eyes.

"No...no, no—for everyone to be happy. It won't ever happen."

"I suppose you're right, and I suppose that's why I make such a lofty offer. Deep down, I know that He would never accept such a deal." Joseph stopped and pointed up at the sky before returning his faze toward me with a slight frown plastered across his face.

Joseph continued, "You're a smart young man, Martin—smarter than most people here in the Valley."

"Young man? But I'm just a boy."

"You're more of a man than most of the men I know. Besides, how old are you now?"

"I just turned seventeen," I responded.

"See, you're practically an old man like me. Well, you enjoy your day, Martin. Stay out of trouble, or Otto will probably whip you silly. I'm just joking! See ya now. Remember, *carpe diem, quam minimum credula poster.* One day, you'll yearn to be youthful again. When does a boy become a man? Now, that's a hard question to answer, isn't it? Does the boy decide, or is he simply a boat being dragged by the unrelenting current into adulthood? Slowly but surely, his innocence is stripped away until there is nothing left but rigid bone. He..."

Joseph continued to ramble as he dragged his dainty cart off into the Valley of Ashes. He wobbled with every step he took. He left with a sudden lurch, unaware he had started walking the way he came instead of the way he was going before he had stopped to talk to me. He'd figure it out eventually.

Joseph had been right. Slowly but surely, I felt my understanding of the Valley change in extraordinary ways. My innocence diminished with each setting of the sun.

A week before, I had witnessed murder for the first time. From my window, I watched as a man fired three shots into the chest of the owner of a small shop that stood next to Wilson's Garage. Within ten minutes, his body was swept away before any reporters or policemen could arrive to investigate. A mind like mine became numb to murder, especially after witnessing many more, but for some reason, the first one always sticks. The rest are much easier to watch...

Chapter 3

From my window, I watched the mosquitoes dance about the massive puddles that had formed overnight.

When it rained, the Valley endured a thick, syrupy humidity that drove people insane—*absolutely* insane.

Someone had told me once that the rate of crime and car accidents spiked on summer days that followed heavy rainstorms. This factoid could have been nothing more than a tall tale made up by an inventive statistician, but I believe, for good reasons now, this fact to be nothing but the truth. Something about the humidity drove people crazy; you could see it in their eyes and the way their bodies moved; they lacked purpose and restraint.

The nighttime rain had stained the dirt outside my window a licorice-tainted brown, leaving puddles of murky water scattered throughout the Valley. Deep ruts ran haphazardly through the dirt roads like several railroad tracks meeting at a complex junction. The overinflated tires of cars, trucks, and wagons spun through the mud as people fought to reach their destinations in a timely fashion, not wanting to be late as they sped away from their soaked shanties. The Valley of Ashes came to life on that hot, humid summer morning.

A piercing chill traveled down my spine as I remembered that I was not the only one keeping watch over the Valley of Ashes. My eyes met a strange sight, yet one that matched the bleakness of the Valley.

A pair of painted eyes, shielded by a pair of wire-framed glasses, stared into my soul, judging my existence as I joined them in gazing down upon the Valley. The eyes lacked a proper nose of their own, but they watched every other nostrilled creature that passed. The eyes never spoke but condemned the wicked people with an icy gaze. Most people never noticed *him* up there as they were busy living their lives, oblivious to their creator's towering presence.

Those sullen, judgmental eyes belonged to Doctor T. J. Eckleburg, an optometrist who hid away in an office somewhere in the heart of Queens. Most people back then assumed he had died—but those who knew him knew he was very much alive.

A thin coat of ash covered the billboard's blue paint that had begun to chip and peel from years of exposure to the elements. Otto told me they had put it up on a Monday, and at first, the fresh blue paint glistened in the sun, but a week later, the ash had covered the billboard, stripping it of its freshness.

They never came to repaint the billboard either—it advertised a service most in the Valley never needed or if they did, had no means of affording.

Doctor T.J. Eckleburg's eyes greeted the trains and cars that entered and exited the Valley, but no one ever returned his silent salutations. Those passing through the Valley who could afford his services were too busy inspecting our misery to notice the billboard staring down on them, judging them as much, if not more, than the people of the Valley.

The blue eyes of the billboard lacked a corresponding mouth, but I liked to imagine if there were one, it would be a smile—a superficial one that slightly jerked to one side, as if someone held a gun to his head, forcing him to smile.

Although his expression showed no hint of malevolence, he lacked any power to enact meaningful change. Instead, he stood by and watched as the world gradually corrupted itself, unable to save his creation but relieved that his position spared him from the destruction unfolding before him.

Shortly before the War, Doctor T. J. Eckleburg immigrated to the United States through Ellis Island, packed full of Europeans trying to escape a poverty-stricken life. I suppose they believed that a life of poverty in the United States was preferable to a life of poverty in their native country, but was it really?

However, the doctor was out of place among those wayward travelers; he belonged to a distinguished class of men. His older brother, a big shot in the new government back in Germany, had maneuvered his way into power shortly after the War ended. His younger brother, who had been a soldier in the German Army, crossed paths with a stray bullet ten minutes before the armistice went into effect. They never found his body after the War ended.

How did I know all of this? Well, Otto told me everything, of course. He always told me everything, anything I wanted to know. Otto always knew a little more about people than he probably should have; he would have made a great detective in a different life.

When Otto wasn't working, he split his time between Winebrenner's poolroom and whatever other speakeasy he could find in the City. With a little bit of alcohol in their systems, people will tell you all about themselves—especially things they shouldn't be telling you.

One day, while sitting in Winebrenner's, Doctor T. J. Eckleburg sat down right next to Otto, his eyes and glasses identical to his billboard caricature. The doctor downed a whole decanter of whiskey and told Otto his entire life story without a single hesitation, explaining to him all of the problems he faced dealing with enigmatic patients and the illicit lifestyle that brought them immense wealth.

I suppose anxious patients also told their optometrist things they shouldn't tell ordinary people, especially when they were the bosses of some of the most well-known organized crime syndicates in the tri-state area. Doctor T. J. Eckleburg had found a niche clientele, and he had moved off the grid, albeit for the forgotten billboard in the Valley of Ashes.

Otto loved to yap, but he also knew when to shut up, especially if he was hearing something he knew he shouldn't be listening to—or something that would benefit him later on. There was plenty of that type of talk happening in the places he frequented; politicians, bootleggers, flappers, and ordinary people spilled their stories after only a few rounds of drinks. The world had run dry, but a flood of mischief had nurtured the cracked earth back to life.

Otto never drank all that much—at least not in front of me. He preferred smoking his cigars—he was absolutely a law-abiding citizen, he had frequently assured me. He only visited those speakeasies to listen and learn about the strange men and women who lived around us. There was an infinite supply of them in this part of the country. That was for sure.

4

Chapter 4

Carl had always been one of my only friends. We were like two piers of a bridge. If one crumbled, the whole bridge came tumbling down. Therefore, we stuck together through thick and thin as best as we could.

Back when we were still attending Adam Smith Memorial School, I had explained to him my scheme to be rich one day and escape the Valley of Ashes. His eyes glowed when I told him the details of my plan to one day move to Paris after amassing my wealth, leaving the dusty Valley—well, in the dust. Carl wanted out of the Valley just as much as I did, and he'd do anything to help me get us out of there.

Carl, with his brawn and unwavering support of my plan, was the perfect person to assist me in my venture. I couldn't even finish asking him before he jumped to his feet, eager to help me in any way he could. I needed someone to help me haul a crate of oranges from Wallabout Market back to the Valley, and Carl was someone I could trust.

We hadn't always been the best of friends, but gone were the days when we'd get into petty arguments and go weeks without talking to one another—at least, I had thought those days were gone. For the most part, that behavior had died when we left school.

Sometimes, the arguments were over what we would be doing after school; sometimes, it would be about who was the smartest, and sometimes, it was about a girl—those were the worst arguments of all.

Most times, he forgave me in the end; however, it was usually out of necessity, stemming from the fact he needed Otto and me to protect him from the wicked lynchers that roamed the streets of the Valley like blood-thirsty hyenas.

One time, Carl and I were in an argument over our classmate's twin sister. Her name was Penelope.

She was a pretty girl, not the prettiest girl I had ever seen, but pretty enough to make someone stop and stare for a little longer than they should.

She almost always wore blue—a light, baby blue like a cloudless sky on a warm spring day. It had been her favorite color for as long as I had known her, and she displayed it every chance she had. It complimented her green eyes splendidly.

She had cut her hair to the bob style of the day, but she lacked the pencil thinness of a true flapper. Prettiest of all were her eyes, round like marbles, with only a two-inch gap between them. She never left the house without her glasses.

She was much more than just a pretty object to look at; her intellect far surpassed that of Carl and me combined.

Unfortunately, her competent mind, made of weakened glass, often shattered at the most minor offense.

In those days, men feared a girl who outpaced them in academics and common sense, but I had long admired Penelope's brains. My father was one of those men who was always scared that some woman would put him in his place.

Penelope was a liberated woman, the norm for the time. I disregarded her elusiveness due to the sheer fact that she was the only girl who paid attention to me while I was in school.

She'd often walk home with her brother Hank after school emptied for the day. On days that I was able to muster the energy to say hello, she responded with a matching hello at best. Most of the time, she was distracted by another boy that her brother was bringing home.

Our parents had been good friends. They lived near Wallabout Market, and we lived here in the Valley. When we were younger, we used to frolic through whatever empty field we could find on the edges of the Valley. We were still the same height then—so much has changed since then.

At that time, we were still unaware of the wasteland that consumed us as we played. That was when life didn't matter and hadn't grabbed us both by the necks, yanking us in opposite directions.

Carl and I went back and forth for a month, arguing about who had the right to marry her. At the time, she knew little of her attractiveness and had no clue about the fights she caused.

Little did we know she had a boyfriend at the time of the argument, something we had failed to consider prior to engaging in our battle. When we went to war over a girl, Carl and I were blind to the destruction and casualties that resulted from our dispute.

In the midst of our engagement, Carl had no choice but to capitulate when he knocked on our front door one night, asking Otto if he could stay for the night. He looked like a scared raccoon, crouching and looking over his shoulder as if someone was waiting to drag him into the darkness of the night.

Carl's eyes twitched, and he frowned as Otto stood in the doorway, contemplating whether or not to let him stay for the night. Sweat dribbled down Carl as he tried to catch his breath, grabbing at his collar to fan himself off. His clothes were smeared with dirt and ash; a few fresh cuts covered his chin and cheeks. Fresh blood oozed from his wounds.

We quickly ascertained that a group of Irish men were going around harassing people in the Valley of Ashes, looking to cause some trouble. Earlier that day, Carl had foolishly picked a fight with an Irish boy and had broken that boy's nose into a million pieces. That boy happened to be the son of one of these nasty Irish men, and they wanted revenge for the pummeling of the Irish boy.

As I already explained, Otto wasn't too thrilled about it, but he eventually reached a compromise with Carl that allowed him to stay the night on one condition—he needed to clean the house. He gave Carl a fist-sized sponge and made him wipe down the entire exterior of the house.

It would have been better for Otto to have given Carl something to do inside, keeping him hidden in case the Irish men walked by, but Otto didn't worry about it. While Carl washed the house, Otto sat in his rocking chair, reading his German newspaper and puffing away on one of his favorite cigars. He told me if those Irish men tried bothering us, he'd tell them he had hired Carl for a job. Otto wasn't intimidated by a couple of amateur thugs.

* * *

Carl snuck up on me as I daydreamed about a future far away from the Valley, somewhere that had clean air and palatable water. His large hands grabbed my shoulders, and he shook me.

He had promised to meet me on the edge of the Valley as soon as his parents left for work. Like me, he also wore his favorite pair of overalls and a loose-fitting worker's cap.

"Are we going to get going? The sun's already up," Carl said, pointing to the sky. "This plan of yours better work. My boss hit me over the head yesterday with a two-by-four, and I'm just—if I don't leave this place soon, I'm going to lose it."

"You're the one that's late. I've been waiting for the past ten minutes for you to show up," I said as I checked the time on the watch that my sister had given me for my birthday.

"You know, I was just joking. I didn't actually get hit in the head by a two-by-four, but I really am getting sick of this place. I want to see the world, Martin, and I know you do too."

I wasn't about to tell him that selling a single crate of oranges wasn't going to get us to Paris. It was going to be a slow and steady grind. First, it would be a crate of oranges, and then slowly, we would build our way up to an industrial empire that produced cars, soap, food, and everything else under the sun.

"My parents warned me not to help you with your business, but they don't know you like I do. You're a smart guy; you have all of this figured out already, I bet. By tomorrow, we'll be the richest fellas in the Valley," Carl said.

"Carl, I don't think we're going to get—"

"It will be great. Maybe I can even buy something nice for Penelope."

I froze.

"Penelope? Like *the* Penelope? Hank's sister? The one we spent a month arguing over? P-E-N-E-L-O-P-E? Penelope?"

"Yes! That's her! Crazy, right? It turns out she broke up with her boyfriend last year. I saw her walking down the road alone one day, and I stopped to say hi. One thing led to another, and we've been dating for a few months now. We'll probably get married next spring as long as things keep going the way they are."

My eyes widened as I tried to determine whether Carl was telling the truth about marrying her. I considered lashing out at him for violating the terms of our informal white peace, but I decided to wave the white flag instead, letting him take the victory. It wasn't worth angering Carl. He wasn't someone you wanted to make angry, and I needed his help.

"Is it serious?" I asked.

"What?"

"You and Penelope?"

"Oh, yeah—I guess. As I said, we're going to get married soon, maybe this spring, when the flowers start to blossom in the fields beyond the Valley. Also, there is something else…"

"What? What else could there possibly be?" I said, crossing my arms.

"Well…She…"

"What? She what? Spit it out!"

"She's pregnant."

My eyes widened once again. "Pregnant?! Like, with a baby?"

Carl rolled his eyes. "No, with a crocodile—of course, with a baby!"

Clearly, the news was still raw for Carl; I would have reacted the same way if I were him. I was more than pleased not to be him at that moment.

We both went silent. The only noise came from the birds that squawked violently above us, as well as Carl's heavy breathing. I had no idea how to console him or if I even wanted to. Truthfully, nothing I could say would have made his dim reality any better.

"How does Penelope…feel about it?" I said carefully, not wanting to upset him any further.

"Well…she's looking forward to being a mother, I guess, but she thinks I'll be a terrible father. I don't have a good job, I'm too young, and I still live in the Valley with my parents."

"Those are all very true," I said with a chuckle.

Carl shot me an angry look, but it quickly vanished as he realized that I was right.

"I assured everything's going to be alright, though. I told her about your plan—your plan to get us rich. I told her we'd be living in a mansion out in West Egg in no time."

"In no time?"

"Yeah, you said we'd be rich, Martin. We'll be alright, right?"

"*Right.* Yes—of course. We'll be alright," I said as I scratched the back of my head.

I refused to promise Carl anything that I couldn't guarantee him. However, at that moment, I felt some sort of…social responsibility to him now that he was going to be a father. I hated it.

I had no intention of telling Carl that my business plan was not guaranteed to succeed. That would only make him upset and possibly bail on me.

Plenty of businesses failed before they even started. We were no better than the rest, and we had a lot of work in front of us. However, I admired his desperation in light of his new circumstances and planned to exploit every ounce of motivation he had as the day progressed.

Carl started again, "Penelope's been nagging me about the future—about what it will look like. 'I have no crystal ball,' I keep telling her. Every waking minute, she'll talk my ear off about how neither of us is ready to be a parent."

"At least you don't have to deal with her today while you're here with me."

"You're right. I'm lucky I get to avoid her for the day. Knowing her, I'm surprised she hasn't found a way to hook a telephone line to me, making me drag it all around the Valley. That way, she'd be able to reach me whenever she thought she needed to. Thankfully, that would never work; someone would cut that cord as soon as they tripped over it," Carl said with a laugh.

"Now, that would be pure torture, having to be on call constantly. I'd go insane."

"I think everyone would. That's why no one's done it yet. Telephones are annoying enough; no need to make them portable."

I was no stranger to Penelope's nagging and her desire for a grander life that neither of us could provide her. Both of us were boys stuck in the binds of the Valley of Ashes and couldn't possibly be the answer to all of her problems.

She wasn't from the Valley, but her family lived an almost identical life to Otto and I. She lived over by Wallabout Market. Her parents worked on the docks, unloading ships and trucks as they arrived from all over the world.

Some day, she planned to escape, just as we all did, but I was seen as a barrier to this dream.

Her smile, infectious like a terminal disease, had the combustive power to ignite a fire in the dampest of downpours. This, along with her craftiness, brought her in contact with wealthy young gentlemen at parties out on West Egg. They had no clue that she lacked the social or financial status that they would have preferred; they admired the lovely view—that's all.

She abused the lust of these young men to get into these parties that drew wealthy socialites, Senators, bootleggers, and more. However, she didn't dare to bring Carl, for he'd spoil the ripe bunch that she had spent precious time cultivating.

"So, what have you been up to for work?" I asked.

"Different things," Carl said, shrugging his shoulders.

"Like?"

"All types of—things."

"Things? What things?"

"It's just—too many jobs to list out….that's all. I've been working so many jobs; I'm saving money for the baby."

"Oh, okay. I was just curious."

As we continued on our way toward Wallabout Market, we passed by a few boys playing baseball in an abandoned lot on the edge of the Valley, half-corrupted yet free from any infant ash heaps.

Bushes, void of lush summer leaves, hugged the fence line, harboring families of ticks and termites. The empty ball field, once home to an ammunition factory, had a sign that read *Stop Do Not Enter Private Property*. Half the boys in the Valley of Ashes couldn't read, so that sign meant nothing to them. They played on.

"You'd think they'd know they can't play here," I said, turning Carl's attention to the game.

"What else are they supposed to do for fun?"

"Fun. Who needs fun, Carl? Not us, right?" I asked sarcastically.

"No, not us. We're businessmen. No fun in that," Carl answered, picking up on my game.

The children used empty sacks of flour for bases, a wooden broom handle as a bat, and, lacking a proper baseball, a wad of rubber that one of the boys had probably found in a pile of trash somewhere in the Valley.

Thousands of telegraph messages zipped through the Valley of Ashes as they darted between Long Island and the City. A steady buzz came from the lines that hung over our heads. Sometimes, the boys' make-shift ball became trapped in the jungle of wires.

A few sad trees lined the edge of the empty field, marking the left-field foul line. Soon enough, the trees' dead leaves would fall like ashes raining down from the smokestacks of the many factories that dotted the Valley, corrupting the land they occupied. Right field emptied into the busy road.

There was a runner on second and third base. A boy about the size of a broomstick rocked as he waited for the pitcher to wind up. As the rubber ball sailed towards home plate, the batter swung, making contact and driving the ball high into the sky.

A column of cars drove by, honking as one of the outfielders chased after the ball as it bounced across the road and into traffic. The two runners on base sprinted home, and the batter stopped as he reached third base. His teammates cheered as they took the lead.

Soon, it would be winter, and the children, who were too young to be pulled into work, would be chucking icy snowballs at each other, waging a make-believe war over unknown aims. However, these snowballs were not white like milk. Their ammunition was an oily black, stained by the ash that continued to arrive year-round from the never-sleeping city.

We kept walking, slowly making our way to Wallabout Market. Carl smiled at all of the pretty girls that walked by. Sometimes, he even gave them a wave, as if Penelope didn't even exist in his mind.

A boy, not much older than us, walked by us with a tennis magazine tucked under his arm. On the cover, a young woman with a blonde bob looked out at us as if she needed our help. Her two delicate hands wrapped softly around her tennis racket, which she held out in front of her.

"Look there," I said to Carl.

"Where?"

"There. The magazine. Look at the cover."

"What about it? Who is that?"

"That's Jordan Baker."

"And she is…?"

"The famous tennis player. Come on. Every man in this city would die to go on a date with her."

"Never heard of her," Carl said, shaking his head.

Otto had met Jordan Baker once at the same place where he met all of the interesting people he knew: a speakeasy. She was there with some young, new-money Wall Street type, bored out of her mind with one hand holding up her head, thinking of another man for sure. Otto didn't have the chance to talk to Miss Baker directly that day, but he sensed that she wouldn't be interested in having a conversation with him anyway. He wasn't her type.

"She was one of the liberated ones," Otto had told me. "She was clueless about the world, yet expected everyone and anything to bend to her invented reality. She was of the new age—the future American, some people say."

Carl turned his head towards me and said with a smile, "My little brother started school the other day."

"How does he like it?" I asked.

"He likes his teacher so far, and he hasn't been attacked by his classmates yet, so I guess that's a plus."

"You think he'll make it any further than we did?" I asked as I looked Carl in the eyes, remembering how he had looked when we had been in school. His overall facial features remained unchanged, but he was half a foot taller, towering over my smaller frame.

"I'm not sure how far he'll make it. My brother can barely spell his name, and he can't read a thing. My parents can't teach him because they don't know how to read or write. Both of their parents, my grandparents, were illiterate too; no chance they were going to teach their kids any reading or writing."

"That's true," I said.

School had been alright for the little time that we were there. We stopped going once we turned fifteen, opting to go to work instead in hopes of making it out of the Valley faster than the suckers who chose to stay in school. I made some friends and learned a bunch of sophisticated words, but otherwise, school had been a waste of my time.

"I hope he never has to put up with Mr. Hinkle. However, I would give anything to go back to that time of my life."

I nodded in agreement, remembering a time when life didn't seem so difficult.

"Mr. Hinkle was a horrible teacher."

"—And an even worse human being," Carl sneered.

Mr. Hinkle had been the last teacher Carl and I had before we stopped going to school.

"Remember, he had that affair with one of his students' mother?" Carl asked.

"Oh, I sure remember that. I know she wasn't married, but man, that wasn't good."

"The Dean acted like he had no idea what was going on, but every student, even the most naive of us, knew what was going down behind closed doors—a *lot* was going down."

"That's all people talked about for that entire school year."

"He was an old man who lunged at the opportunity to relive his younger years, unaware that the train had long left the station," Carl said with a laugh and a roll of his eyes.

"Remember when he tried telling us once that it was the Union's fault for starting the Civil War? To him, *his* South was innocent."

"Wasn't he from Georgia, too?"

"Yes! He was!" I blurted out, shaking my head.

Carl turned and asked me, "If we were so guilty, why'd he even move to New York in the first place? Why didn't he stay put in Georgia?"

I rubbed my chin and searched for a neutral answer before saying, "Well, maybe he lives in a nice part of New York," I stopped to consider if that was even a real place and then continued, "He'd run all the way back to the coast of Georgia if he had to live with us here in the Valley. He wouldn't last a day living here."

Carl smirked. "I guess you're right. He'd much rather live in Georgia than stay up here in the Valley surrounded by filthy boys like us."

"Well, I don't know about that one. Even in Georgia, he'd still have to live with people like you. But that'd be better than teaching a bunch of kids from the Valley, I guess. Eventually, all of our ash would make him look just like…"

Carl stopped dead in his tracks, grabbed both of my arms with his fat hands, and lifted me off my feet. Shaking me in the air, he roared, "What you mean people like me? He'd look just like a *what*?"

At that moment, if he had decided to throw me to the ground, he could have killed me. I was unable to spit out an answer as adrenaline rushed through my body. I kicked my legs helplessly as he continued to hold me up in the air.

"You've been spending too much time around that stupid old man. He's been reading all that garbage that says I'm going to eat people's babies cause I don't look like them. Do I look like I'd eat a baby, Martin?"

He was right. I was not too fond of the stuff Otto read, but I guess Otto had rubbed off on me a bit somehow.

"I'm sorry, Carl. I didn't mean it like that."

Reluctantly, Carl placed me back down on the ground after realizing I wasn't ever going to give him the answer that he really wanted. I refused to admit that he was right, but I knew I'd be taking an unnecessary risk by not apologizing to him.

It didn't matter. Carl knew he was right; otherwise, he wouldn't have put me back on my feet.

We walked a few miles in silence, but Carl didn't stray far from my side despite our quick scuffle. He knew that without me, he'd be stuck in the Valley of Ashes forever, shoveling ash as it arrived in carts from the city, unable to ever please Penelope. He needed me if he ever wanted to leave.

And to answer his question, while he didn't look like he'd eat a baby, I remember being afraid he was going to rip me out of my desk and throw me out the window the first time he sat down next to me in school. I eventually got over my fear, but I always knew that Carl would be capable of violence if someone ever pushed him to it, and it didn't take too much to push him over the edge.

Finally, Carl broke the silence, "Where are we even going?"

"Wallabout Market"

"Walla—what?"

"Wallabout Market. Don't worry, Carl. We're almost there. My parents brought me there once when I was little. It's a bustling place."

Carl nodded as if he approved of my brief description of the operation that went on at Wallabout Market. In all honesty, my parents had never taken me there.

I made the whole story up. I knew if I told Carl the truth, he would abandon me in my adventure.

I didn't even know where the market was. I mainly relied on the vague directions that Otto had reluctantly given me after some pleading.

"So, we're just selling fruit? That's it? That's your plan to get rich?" Carl asked.

"Yes, I've saved up enough to buy a crate of oranges. We're going to sell them to drivers and their passengers as they drive through the Valley."

Carl scratched his chin as he thought about how he could add more to the venture but struggled to come up with any meaningful contribution.

As Carl continued to rack his brain, we passed by two Irish boys chit-chatting at the intersection of two narrow streets. They clearly were not from the Valley; their skin, smooth like a spread of margarine, lacked the tinge given by the ash. I instantly felt the sting of their glare as they sized us up, deciding how easy it would be to take us down.

The two boys were about the size of Carl; both of them towered over me and had twice the muscle mass I had. They focused on Carl more than they did me, realizing that he posed the more significant threat. Eventually, one of the boys recognized who I was and stomped up to me like a soldier preparing to raid an enemy trench.

Those Irish boys never bothered me before, and I figured they wouldn't bother roughing me up this time around. Otto used to tell me that as long as they knew I was staying with him, they wouldn't lay a single finger on me. I never asked him why, but I felt a lot safer roaming the streets, knowing that dropping Otto's name somehow protected me.

"What are you doing walking around with a boy like him?" the taller of the two boys yelled at me while pointing at Carl.

I ignored the boy's question.

"Keep walking," I muttered to Carl.

"You heard me, didn't you? What are you doing walking around with a boy like him? Don't make me ask you again."

I turned to face the boy and tucked my right hand into my overalls.

"You know who I am. I'm Martin Köhler. Leave us alone if you know what's good for you."

That should have been clear enough of a message to send them running, but it didn't work.

The two Irish boys didn't back down. They stood still, cautious but ready to strike at a moment's notice. I started to worry a little but brushed it off, keeping my cool.

I pointed towards Carl. "You mess with him, and you mess with not only me but also Otto Schulze. You don't want to mess with Otto. Do you?"

I hoped that was enough context to save me from a fight. For such a dull man, Otto maintained a strikingly high level of respect throughout the Valley. Dropping his name had gotten me out of a lot of trouble in the past.

The boy took a step back, looked at his friend, and shrugged his shoulders, dismissing my words.

"We don't care. He's not here right now. We'll take our chances."

Suddenly, the smaller but more rough-looking boy launched into a tirade of racial expletives.

They appeared unfazed by the threat of Otto as the tirade of words continued.

The other boy looked as though he was ready to put us ten feet under. He cracked both sets of knuckles and dropped his coat to the ground.

I turned to Carl and yelled, "Run."

We booked it as fast as we could, kicking dust up under our feet. We kept looking over our shoulders, waiting for one of the boy's hands to come down on us.

The smaller one was still flapping his mouth, oblivious to the fact that we had departed, but he quickly joined his friend, who had started chasing after us.

Carl was a lot faster than me, and I struggled to keep up with his long strides.

Suddenly, my foot collided with a rock sticking out of the ground.

My arms flailed.

I gasped.

I tumbled forward, accidentally taking Carl down to the ground with me.

As I spit out the dirt that had entered my mouth, the footsteps of the boys approached us with a menacing roar.

We were dead, for sure. One of the boys stood over me; he wound his arm back as he prepared to deliver his first blow to my head.

His sweat dripped down onto my face. I was paralyzed and unable to wipe my face free from the foreign substance.

However, as I turned my head towards the approaching stampede, the boys first stopped as if they had hit an invisible wall.

The taller boy looked around, orientating himself to where he was. After realizing just how far they had chased us, they looked at each other.

They stared at each other blankly. The shorter boy's mouth hung open. They turned and ran as if an invisible hand was chasing them.

Carl and I looked at each other, stunned by the sudden fear that the boys had expressed. Then we both saw what they had seen.

A few men in suits stood outside of a shabby drugstore, watching us struggling in the mud. I looked their way for a moment as they lifted their hands from their overcoats. Half-expecting them to produce a weapon of some sort, I was disappointed when their hands emerged empty, holding nothing but the tense air.

My eyes met the ominous glare of one of the men; his eyes were empty, void of any feeling. He gave me a slight nod before ducking back into the drugstore, never to be seen again. In his right hand, he held a corked bottle; it glistened in the sun.

The man looked familiar, but I couldn't tell where I had seen him before. The other men with him looked around and retreated inside, locking the door behind them.

We got up and tried cleaning our mud-covered clothing. Carl bent over, placing his hands on his knees as he breathed heavily.

I gasped for air, too.

We both coughed as our lungs refused to cooperate, leaving us feeling lightheaded and tired. Our chests expanded and contracted as we sucked more oxygen into our bloodstream. I felt lightheaded.

Ash had infiltrated our lungs a long time ago, rendering them nearly useless when under heavy stress. We sat down on the ground for a moment as we recovered. After our heavy breathing subsided, we got up and made sure that no one was watching us. The streets had emptied.

"What was that about?" Carl asked with wide eyes.

"I—I don't know. I've seen them before. They usually walk up to me, and then I'll remind them that I know Otto, and they continue right on their merry way."

"They didn't seem to care about Otto."

"No, they didn't, did they? It's not that they didn't remember. They didn't seem to care," I said.

"Strange and even stranger that they just stopped out of nowhere. Maybe they all of a sudden remembered who Otto was," Carl suggested.

"I don't know—they'd have to be awfully slow to take that long to remember, but it doesn't matter anymore. They won't be back. Let's get going; we're almost to the market—I hope."

Chapter 5

Thousands of wooden crates, barrels, and people occupied the never-ending labyrinth of Wallabout Market. Men, some short and stout, others tall and slim, sold everything from fresh fish to crates of McIntosh apples. As the sun beat down on the men, they sought refuge in the sparse shadows cast by trucks and a few building's facades.

Workers rushed about the market, unloading bins from the ships as they arrived in the harbor and transferring them to the vendors that waited for them. Two cranes, each about two stories high, unloaded produce onto the bustling dock below. Their arms swung like two drunken men fighting in a speakeasy.

In the middle of the dock, Penelope's father, Albert, unloaded boxes of apples and pears. In between each heave, he slicked back his greasy salt and pepper hair. Sweat covered his palms as he wiped his face dry.

I greeted him with a gentle wave of my hand, but he continued his daily duties, unaware of my presence. Otto had always praised him, and that was something Otto rarely did for any man. In the past, Penelope had worked with her father in the market, but that day, to my disappointment, she was nowhere to be found.

Perhaps, now that she was pregnant, she no longer felt capable of working at the market, I thought to myself. I could have used her that day. She would have understood my business plan better than most.

Carl and Otto only passively lauded my dream, while Penelope would have understood and joined me in dreaming. Secretly, she had hoped that I could one day rescue her from her melancholy life.

I could have asked Carl where she was for the day, but I didn't want him to think that I was stuck thinking about his girl. Had I known ahead of time that they were together, I would have asked Carl to bring her just so that I could see her once again.

Carl and I looked out of place among the older men, but most of them were too busy to notice us walking through the crowded market. As we tried to find a vendor selling oranges, my ears were bombarded by noises from every direction. A medley of accents shouted the shared vocabulary of business.

Sold.
No.
Money.
Yes.
Please.
Please.

Please.

Butchers, clad in stained smocks, laid out slaughtered livestock for all that passed by to see. A pungent smell of fresh blood wafted through the air. I pinched my nose.

Crates of vegetables and fruits rolled past us on wooden carts. We peered into the bins to see if any of them carried oranges, but they were all missing the fruit that we desired. We had a particular taste.

Everyone and everything moved at peak efficiency throughout the entire market.

A lapse in efficiency meant a loss in revenue.

A loss in revenue meant a loss in profit.

A loss in profit meant the imminent death of their enterprise.

"Martin, this is incredible. Look at all of these people! This place is a madhouse!"

"I know, amazing, right? Who knew that the City consumes this much food? Now we just have to find someone who's selling some oranges."

"How about we split up? Then we'll find each other once one of us finds someone selling oranges."

I hesitated.

"Sure, sounds like a plan. Just don't get lost on me. I can't lose you this early in the day."

Carl and I walked off in different directions. I made my way through the crowd like a boat navigating rough waters, riding the waves of people as they jolted me back and forth. Their elbows dug into me as I collided with them.

Then, after searching the market for about twenty minutes, I finally found a vendor selling oranges. He had about one hundred crates stacked in piles, five by five by two.

Two men with funny mustaches and matching hats carried a single crate by me, struggling as they made their way towards their truck.

Halfway, they dropped the crate and stretched their fingers and arms before picking it up again. One of the men glanced down at me with an emotionless gaze before averting his eyes away in a hurry. After loading the crate into the back of their truck, they quickly hopped in and sped off, kicking up a cloud of dust behind them.

I returned my focus to the task at hand. I stood up straight and puffed up my chest in an attempt to look older than I actually was, wanting the man to take me seriously. I looked into one of the crates; the oranges, round and ripe, were ideal for selling.

"How much for a crate?" I asked as I pointed to one of the crates.

"Sorry, kid, you have to buy twenty crates. Can't just buy one," the vendor responded as he shook his head.

"But I only want one crate."

"You have to buy twenty. No exceptions. That's the rule."

"What rule?

"My rule. Now beat it."

"But those guys just bought one—"

He held up his worn hand. "I don't have time for you kid. Either you buy twenty crates, or you can go pound sand. I don't deal with people like you."

"Can't I just buy one crate? Please," I begged.

The vendor shook his head as he returned to rearranging his crates. I was about to plead again when I felt a hand clutch my shoulder.

"Charlie, I'll buy the kid a crate and add it to my usual order. No problem at all, right?" a menacing voice said from behind me.

Without hesitation, the vendor placed a crate on the ground for me. Charlie gave a slight bow to the man standing over my shoulder.

I whipped around and looked up at the man while smiling, grateful for the gracious deed he had done for me.

A large, hat-covered head sat on his two broad shoulders like a monkey perched on a branch. He wasn't fat, but his immense size created a power imbalance between us, like a man staring up at God.

His whiskey-tinged breath diffused across my face every time that he exhaled. A layer of dirty sweat covered his wrinkled forehead. It was the hottest day of the year, after all.

"Thank you, sir. I'm starting a fruit stand, and I—"

The mysterious man cut me off with a wave of his hand, "Not a problem, my boy. I understand completely. I run a very successful—restaurant in the City. I also send five crates of these oranges to my dear friend out in West Egg every weekend—a fine gift for a fine gentleman, don't you think?"

"Yes, sounds like a great gift. I'm surprised he uses that many oranges in a single weekend."

"Ah yes, he throws many…functions. Uses them all up in a single night. I admire your entrepreneurial mind, especially at such a young age. It reminds me of my youth. You know I may have a business connection for you—how old are you?"

His thick yet understandable accent, reminiscent of Otto's tongue, masked something sinister—his cuff links were made of molars that appeared to originate from a monkey or ape…or something else entirely. His physique matched Otto's stereotypical descriptions of the type of people to watch out for, but I ignored Otto's warnings as they rang through my head, becoming intoxicated by the man's bubbly spirit.

"I just turned seventeen. I—I'll almost be eighteen, though," I answered him as I once again puffed up my chest to make myself appear older.

He took two steps back and looked around worriedly as if he had become allergic to my presence. "Never mind, forget I said anything about that. It was nice meeting you, though, Martin. Good luck with your fruit stand."

He reached into his puffy overcoat and pulled out a crumpled business card made of thin card stock. Placing the card between the palms of his hands, he rubbed it in an attempt to flatten it out.

"Sorry, it is a bit tattered, but here," he said as he handed me his card, "take this in case you ever need to reach me…perhaps when you're a little older."

The card lacked any reference to the man's name but had an address for a company scribbled in ink.

"Thank you very much, Mr…"

"Mr. Wolfsheim. And, of course, the pleasure is mine, Martin."

He extended his wrinkled hand, and I shook it firmly.

After paying Charlie, Mr. Wolfsheim cleared his throat and said, "I must ask you for one favor, though. If anyone asks if you saw me here today, you tell them no, understand?"

"Yes, of course. I'll pretend I never saw you."

Strange, sure, but at the time, I figured that he had blown off a mid-morning date in order to pick up the oranges for his restaurant. He struck me as a devoted businessman, one who put his business before his own needs and those of others. Someone that I could look up to.

"It's a wicked world out there, Martin—but you'll be fine. I know it," Mr. Wolfsheim said with a wink before disappearing into the crush of people.

To my surprise, I was able to lift the oranges myself. They weren't too heavy. At the time, I had no clue why the other men had struggled to pick them up.

I worked my way through the crowd as I tried to find Carl.

Goosebumps rose on my arms.

I looked at the fish stand and the meat counters, but he wasn't there.

I checked the dock, but he wasn't there either.

I started hyperventilating.

My heartbeat soared.

I was suddenly dizzy.

The sun attacked me.

The birds laughed at me as they flew overhead.

After roaming the market for a few more minutes in a state of panic, I found Carl leaning up against a light pole, nonchalantly flirting with a few young girls who were clearly at least twice his age.

He flashed his near-perfect smile and stood with his back all straight. He must have quickly borrowed a man's comb to smooth over his usual disheveled mop. If it weren't for his ratty clothing or his ash-stained skin, he would have fit in with the men down on Wall Street.

As I watched Carl, I wondered if he had forgotten all about Penelope as he flirted with the girls.

I briefly remembered my previous attempts at courting her. They were semi-successful at best, but something kept dragging me along, keeping me in the hunt despite the persistent setbacks. I started to wonder how Carl had managed to infiltrate her impenetrable walls, but I was quickly overcome by bitterness.

"Making Mr. Hinkle proud, are you?" I quipped, attempting to take an ounce of revenge without causing too much damage.

Carl took two giant lunges towards me. I dropped the crate of oranges in front of me. I prepared myself for his worst.

His face sat an inch away from mine. He spoke in a hushed tone so that his new lady friends wouldn't hear my protest.

"What?"

"You know what I said. You think it's right flirting with all of these girls when you got Penelope at home thinking you're out here trying to make a better life for you guys?"

"Oh, I see—you still like her, don't you?" he said, shaking his head.

"No. Of course not."

"It's obvious you're jealous of me."

"I'm not. Never will be."

"Yes, you are. It's obvious. Don't lie to me, or I'll—"

"It doesn't matter if I still like her or not. I won the argument fair and square back when we were in school. We drafted terms. Remember?"

"That was a childish game, Martin. You never made a move, so I stepped in. Go cry about it if you want." Carl grinned.

I wanted to punch him and knock his perfect smile out of his face, but I knew he'd do much worse to me in return.

I looked up at the sun sitting in the sky above us as it inched closer to noon. I shook my head, dismissing any attempt Carl had at continuing his attack, and said:

"Let's go; I got the oranges. I can do this with you or without you. It's up to you."

Carl stopped and calculated my threat.

"Yeah, yeah. Fine. You win. Give me a second to say goodbye to my new friends."

"Friends?" I asked as Carl spun his back on me, returning his attention to the group of girls.

"Goodbye, ladies. Don't forget me, for I may not return from this dangerous journey. When the newspapers print my name, tell the world of my love for the common man—and for you all. Tell them how much I meant to you…and you…and you."

Reluctantly, he departed his newfound lovers, taking each of their hands and kissing them like a gentleman.

He flashed a grin before turning his back on them for good. Carl had a charm about him that he could flip on like a switch. One moment, he showed almost no emotion, and the next, he transformed into a charming gentleman who could woo over the prettiest of princesses from far-off kingdoms.

The girls looked at each other, giggling as he grabbed one side of the crate. I grabbed the other side, and with a quick jolt, we lifted the crate off the ground. Together, we slowly lugged the crate of oranges as we made our way back towards the Valley.

I waited until we were out of earshot of the girls before asking Carl, "Dangerous journey? What was that all about?"

"Well—I told them I was in the Army and that I was about to embark on a secret invasion of some—Latin country. Cool, huh? They were eating up every bit of it, too, but then you came and interrupted the whole thing. I could have had all three of them wrapped around my finger. Maybe we could go back, and I could introduce you to one of them."

"So, you were waiting there the entire time making up stories to those girls?" I asked as I rolled my eyes.

"What's the big deal?"

"Penelope. Penelope's the big deal. Did you forget about her?"

"No, of course not. She goes to her parties, and I flirt with some girls. It's not a big deal."

"Really?"

"Come on, Martin, let's not start another argument. You know we both need each other, or else we'll both be stuck in the Valley forever. Let's forget about Penelope for the day. Deal?"

I bit my tongue, stopping myself from pointing out to him that it was apparent to me that he had already forgotten about her.

"Deal. Whatever."

"So, how much did the crate end up costing you?"

"It didn't cost me anything. I got it for free."

"For free? Did you decide to steal one? Remember what Otto used to tell us: sometimes, if you want to get ahead in life, you have to cheat."

"No. No, I didn't steal it. There was this man—and he bought me the crate," I said as I pointed to the crate of oranges sitting next to me.

"A man? He just bought you a crate of oranges?"

"Miracles happen every day, Carl. We just happened to receive our own. Let's get out of here."

Chapter 6

Children escaped the brutal heat of the midday sun by sitting in a narrow strip of shade cast by the row of decrepit warehouses. They drank water straight from the rusty spigot that hung from the side of the nearby factory building. Wet scraps of cloth hung from their heads, concealing their faces from the suffocating inferno.

"How's your parents, Carl?" I asked.

"Oh, you know—they're alright."

I could sense a lie behind his reassuring words.

"That's the truth?"

"Yes. Yes, they're fine."

"I doubt that. I know when you're lying to me, Carl."

"Fine. I don't think my father has that long left to live." Carl sighed. "There's a tumor about the size of a baseball growing on the back of his head. My mother's been home from work taking care of him."

I understood and didn't ask any further questions. I felt terrible for ripping Carl away from his ailing father to help me, but ultimately, that decision had been made by him, not me.

Sweat trickled down our arms and legs as we carried the crate of oranges through the sweltering streets. It wasn't heavy, but we had about a six-mile walk from the market to the Valley of Ashes. The veins on our arms bulged as blood pumped all through our bodies.

"Hey Martin, Penelope told me she thought she saw Otto at one of those parties out in West Egg."

"Really? She still goes to those *things*?" I asked, half-hoping that he would say no.

"Not as much anymore—only sometimes now that we're together. But, yes, she still goes."

"Does she bring you?"

I would have thought that Penelope's trick would have been discovered after all this time, but she must have carefully rotated her date every time she went, finding a new sucker to roam the party with so that no one would ever catch on to her game.

In Carl, she found stability that none of the rich boys of Long Island ever could, or better, would want to provide. If it weren't for Carl's charm, he'd be just another side character in her large cast of lonely men.

Carl answered, "No, she never brings me along. She says I'd spoil her fun." Realizing what he had just implicated, he continued, "As I said, she doesn't go that often now that we're together, and she promises that I'm better than any of those sleazy, rich guys she meets out at those parties. I'm not much of a party person anyway. Never mind—did you hear what I said? She thought she saw Otto at one of them."

"She saw Otto—at a party? Out on West Egg?"

"That's what she told me. She swears it was him. He wore a nice suit with a bow tie and downed about ten glasses of bubbly before he retired to a private room with a young woman in tow. I guess he cleans up nice."

"Doesn't sound like Otto to me."

"Oh, I'm pretty sure it was. Think about it. He was there, enjoying the free whiskey, the music, and the dancing—and the women. From what she tells me, those parties are to die for."

"I don't think she saw Otto. He wouldn't go to a place like that."

"Do you really know the man? You haven't even lived with him that long. How do you know what he's up to when half the time you're out sneaking around Wallabout Market trying to find Penelope? I know you're—"

"I don't sneak around the market looking for her. That's a lie—a blatant lie. I don't care about Penelope—at least not anymore now that you went ahead and got her pregnant."

If we had gone any further without a break, we would have broken out into total war.

We placed the crate down between us.

Carl crossed his arms.

His eyes narrowed.

I smirked and tapped my foot impatiently, waiting for him to strike first.

Carl lost all emotion in his face, and he looked ready to take a swing at me. I cracked my knuckles, prepared to fend off whatever Carl decided to throw at me.

"Come on, take a swing at me. I know you want to," I taunted.

Carl wound up his right arm and took a swing at my head.

I leaned right; his hand barely clipped my ear.

"This is stupid, Martin. I'm not going to fight you," Carl whined.

"No. No. I know you want to hit me. Go ahead, *big boy.*"

His eyes narrowed once again, but then his body shrunk, returning to a nearly emotionless state.

"No. I'm not going to hit you." He sighed. "I hate to admit it—but without you and your plan, I don't know what I'm going to do."

I nodded my head and grinned. I had won, but at what cost? It didn't matter to me—I had won.

We both took hold of the crate and hoisted it into the air.

"We're almost there, Carl. We're almost there."

* * *

When we made it back to the Valley of Ashes, it was half past noon. The mid-day sun beamed down on the Valley, erasing most of the evidence of the previous night's downpour. Columns of steam shot through the piles of ash like miniature volcanoes. I waited to see an eruption, but one never came.

"So, where are we going to set up shop?" Carl asked as he wiped away a layer of sweat from his forehead and pulled at his shirt collar, combating the unrelenting heat that attacked us from all angles.

"It has to be visible from the main road, and it has to have an area for cars to pull off. Otherwise, no one will stop."

I surveyed the area to find the ideal place. Carl suggested a few spots, but all of them lacked the features we needed.

"Right there," I said as I pointed to a flat area clear of any debris or ash. "As people make their way through the Valley, we'll wave them down. They'll stop and buy some of our oranges. We'll triple our money—they're suckers."

"Do we have a sign?" Carl asked, scratching his head.

"A sign?"

"Yeah, a sign. Every good business has a sign, Martin. Where's ours?"

I had planned everything but somehow had forgotten to make a sign.

After thinking for a moment, I turned to Carl and said, "Go on down to my house, grab a can of paint in my room underneath my bed, and bring it back here. We'll paint the side of the crate instead of making a sign. It will be just as good."

"Alright, I'll be back in ten minutes," Carl said as he turned and jogged down the road towards Otto's house.

The City had been performing repairs on the drawbridge that crossed the Flushing River, linking the Valley of Ashes with the pristine Long Island.

So that they could work on the bridge without interruption, the workers diverted traffic, causing an increase in automobiles venturing into the heart of the Valley.

If I could, I'd pay those workers to keep the bridge closed for the rest of the year. A slight bit of corruption never hurts anyone—especially if no one ever finds out about it.

A train crawled by me as it headed west for Long Island; the next stop was West Egg. As I watched the train roll by, I noticed a familiar face.

Penelope.

Her wandering emerald-colored eyes met mine before being swept away by the anticipation of what awaited her in West Egg. Neither Carl nor I were strong enough to counteract the force that dragged her out there every weekend. Such a force did not be strong with the will she had.

Our eyes locked once again. She flashed a teasing smile, friendly, but nothing more than that. However, her smile nevertheless reignited a fire inside of me that had been extinguished after many nights of mid-summer rain.

She shifted her attention towards the silhouette of a young man sitting next to her. His arm was gently wrapped around her shoulder. I was unable to make out much of him; he resided in the shadows.

As her train passed, she leaned into his embrace. Her lips landed gently on his, but before I could witness much more of the grueling sight, the train slipped away out of the Valley.

Two gunshots went off in the distance. However, I was too flustered to notice fully. My mind wanted to wander, so I let it run.

I was disappointed—no, actually, I felt rather pleased knowing that she had found her escape, even if only temporarily on the weekends. Proud of her? Perhaps.

You could say I felt the same for the young gentleman she had convinced to bring her to the party. Sure, perhaps at the time, I may have been struck with a feeling of jealousy, but I quickly realized that he would have his heart broken too eventually—all with due time.

It was all a part of her cunning plan to escape the Valley. I had my plan, and she had hers; they simply didn't align. She knew that she would never be able to leave the Valley, so she found an alternative way to escape.

I admired her creativity for it all, but I couldn't help but feel bad for Carl at the same time. He deserved better, but he had been simply entranced by the same things that had roped me in years before. He'd get over it—I hoped.

Eventually, Carl returned with a bucket of paint and a brush. I contemplated telling Carl that I had seen Penelope, but I decided against it—for Carl's sake, of course. Instead, I relished in the small affair and returned to business.

"I'm back. I could only find this. Is this what you wanted?" Carl said as he held up a bucket of paint in one hand and a brush in the other.

"Yes. Perfect. Here, set it down."

I took the brush and dipped it in some of the paint—a drip of red splattered on the ground, looking like a smear of blood. After racking my brain for a good name, I wrote *C & M's Clementines* on the long side of the crate.

"Aren't they oranges, not clementines?" Carl asked as he looked at the name.

"It—it has a good ring to it," I answered. "They won't know the difference. They might all be rich, but not all of them are smart."

Carl and I waited on the corner for our first customers. Cars whizzed by us as we finished setting up our shop. We placed a boulder underneath the crate, giving it a slight tilt that allowed the passing motorists to see our oranges.

"Hey Carl, what did you say Penelope was doing today?"

"She was supposed to help her parents clean up around the house."

"Ah, okay," I said, resisting the urge to shake my head in disappointment.

"Why do you ask?"

"No reason. No reason at all."

Carl looked at me; he was curious as to what I was trying to get at. I quickly changed the subject—or at least tried to.

I tried to resist, but I couldn't help myself. I knew it would make Carl mad.

"Hey, Carl. Is she still as beautiful as she was back when we were in school?"

"What?"

"Penelope. You know—like, is she still beautiful now that she's pregnant?"

"I'll throw you off the Brooklyn Bridge if you ask me something stupid like that again."

Before we could launch ourselves into yet another argument, a car squealed to a stop in front of our stand—and then another, and another. Before we knew it, an uncontrollable flood of customers started appearing in front of our stand.

Carl greeted them as they waited patiently in line, using his charm to keep them occupied while I handled the actual selling of the oranges. They were so entranced by his lure that they seemed to forget they were talking to a boy covered head to toe in ash instead of a spiffed-up salesman.

Men in tight suits and hat-wearing women with overdone make-up bought our oranges as if they had never seen such food in their lives.

If I had that kind of money, I would have twenty-two crates of oranges delivered to the Valley every morning. I would set aside ten of them for charity, sending them into the City to the orphanages. The other crates, I'd sell to anyone that drove through the Valley. There was always another dollar to be made, and whether you made that dollar was entirely up to how much more you wanted it compared to the other man.

At my feet, a party of intoxicated mosquitoes drank from the ponds of water left from the nighttime storm. They sucked the life out of the puddles, exposing shallow ruts in the road. The sun also aided in this destructive task. However, a few large puddles remained, refusing to give in to the sun's assault.

Our sales continued into the evening hours as people returned from the City—a coin here and a coin there slowly added up to a small fortune. As we made more sales, my pockets sagged.

Grabbing a small stack of coins, I dumped them into Carl's outstretched hands and told him, "Here is your first cut. Go get yourself something nice after we're done with this."

Carl grinned as he felt the coins roll around his palms. He shoved them deep into his pockets before any nasty birds could swallow them up.

"I think it'd be better for me to save for the baby and share perhaps some with Penelope."

"Oh yeah, I guess you could do that if you wanted to. It's your money now. I—If I could go back just a few years and redo a few days, Penelope would have been mine, not yours, you know that?"

"Martin, I thought I made it clear we weren't going to talk about her again. We weren't going to talk about her for the rest of the day—"

"Put a pause on that deal for a moment, just a moment. We've already violated it multiple times. What is one more violation?"

"Fine. Doesn't matter. Good thing you can't repeat the past," Carl said as he crossed his arms.

"Can't repeat the past? Why, of course, you can, Carl. It's people like you that make it impossible for the rest of us."

"People like me? I make your childish dreams impossible to reach? Learn to live in the present, Martin. You might find yourself happy for once."

Once again, our impending argument was interrupted; a young man driving alone pulled over to the side of the road, hopped out, and walked up to Carl and me as our line began to dwindle. The car's fresh paint job glistened in the sun.

"What are you two boys selling today?" the man asked.

Carl and I exchanged uneasy looks, but I looked at the man and, mocking Carl's charisma, said, "Oranges. We are selling fresh oranges. Today only! Some of the best oranges you can get in New York. Just ask—anybody!"

"They sure look good. I'll take three," the man said as he smiled and pulled out a large wad of bills from his pocket.

One of the three oranges had a spot of mold. I went to grab another orange for the man, but he declined, telling us, "When life is so short, why focus on the little negatives? The inside should be fine."

Before I could explain to him the flaw in his wisdom, he handed Carl and me a few bills each, enough to buy us all out of oranges.

"Keep this; there is no need to give me any change. I remember long ago when I was about your age. I sold candies to my neighbors and to my friends to make my first bit of money. Now look at me," the man said as he looked himself over, flattening his suit against his clean figure as if it were some sign of his success.

The generous man hopped back into his car and sped off down the road, straight for the City. He started a chain reaction. After he left, a line of customers reappeared as more people drove into the City. Most of them were covered in sweat; it was an awfully hot day.

My pockets and my eyes grew heavy. A ten-hour day was no joke, and my body began to let me know that it was unappreciative of the long hours. Of course, the work was much better than anything the ash company would have had me doing. It was the beginning of the life of money-making. I'd be living the good life soon enough—at least, I thought.

We were already down to our last few oranges. I pushed what remained to one side of the crate when I noticed that a few of the bottom boards were loose. I ripped one of the boards out, revealing a bottle full of an amber-colored liquid.

Before I could grab the bottle for further inspection, the sound of a roaring engine erupted behind me. As I spun around, a wave of water splashed over me and my makeshift stand like a monsoon.

My clothes absorbed most of the water, making me drip as the storm subsided. The wave had knocked over what was left in my crate of oranges.

I watched in horror as they rolled into the road. A few of them were immediately squashed by oncoming traffic. I looked left and right for the cause of the sudden disaster.

My eyes landed on a yellow coupe driving down the road toward the City, swerving as it avoided slow-moving vehicles and innocent pedestrians.

"What a bunch of morons!" I muttered under my breath, shaking my head at the stupidity I had just witnessed. Otto was right; some people were just morons.

My eyes slanted, and I shook my head like an out-of-control bobblehead.

"This is all your fault!" I yelled at Carl.

"My fault!?! How is this *my* fault?"

"You should have been looking out for moron drivers—*you* should have told me to watch out."

I dropped to my knees and tried to salvage any oranges that I could, but most were so covered in ash and dirt that they were useless.

I patted my pockets and realized my money had fallen out of my overalls.

I went to gather the scattered bills, but once again, the sound of a rapidly approaching car filled the air.

The engine thumped like an athlete's heartbeat, sprinting toward the finish line. The driver looked like he was prepared to kill any man who stood in his way.

As the driver stepped on the pedal, the engine roared with anger. Just as the yellow car had, this car showed no concern for the safety of pedestrians or fellow drivers. This one, navy blue like the ocean, whizzed by me, nearly turning me into a pancake.

While I was unscathed, the car had hit my money dead on. Its tires mangled my paper money into tiny waterlogged shreds and buried my coins at the bottom of the puddle.

The driver shook his head as if I had been an inconvenience to him. I watched as he banged his hands on the steering wheel. His sweaty hair flapped in the wind.

Thankfully, no one had been crossing the road when they drove by. If there had been someone, they would have been split in half for sure.

My entrepreneurial dreams were dead.

I looked across the ash heaps.

The gigantic eyes of Doctor T.J. Eckleburg looked down upon me. They blinked twice. Despite lacking a proper mouth, he laughed at me like a crooked crow. The wealthy socialites had no care for the destruction they caused in the lives of people like me.

I tried to imagine being stuck in the Valley for the rest of my life, unable to escape as I had intended.

My head spun. My heart pounded; a spark would have made it explode like a firecracker. I tried to control my breathing, but my body refused to quit.

A cloud of dust and ash formed as I launched into a fit of rage, kicking the ground. I refused to be stuck in the Valley for the rest of my life. Otto may have declared the American Dream dead, but I didn't believe in his declaration—not yet.

My skin boiled. Steam poured out from my ears. If I had opened my mouth, a hiss would have pierced the air like a train whistle.

I snapped.

"No. No. No. No."

More clouds of dust formed as I continued pounding the ground with my feet.

I grabbed a board from the destroyed crate and threw it into the traffic. Several cars swerved, avoiding the projectile.

Like a giant, I stomped on the few remaining unscathed oranges, turning them into a chocolate-colored pulp.

"Are you just going to stand there?" I yelled at a frozen Carl.

I shook my head and bolted towards the train station. The train had yet to depart. I took a seat as it began to move.

I peered out the train car's window. Carl stood in the same spot where he had been when the driver destroyed my dreams. He stared at me, amazed at what had occurred. He had no idea the violence I was—never mind.

I couldn't tell if Carl was happy, sad, or something else entirely. Like a stone statue, he lacked emotion. I shook my head at him as if somehow it was his fault, forgetting that he had lost just as much in that moment as I had.

Part Two

Chapter 7

In the heart of the city, skyscrapers grabbed at the clouds above. Their concrete facades, stained brown like shoe polish, lacked inspiration and could have made a grown man cry. At any moment, they threatened to collapse, burying me deep beneath the rubble.

Cars whizzed by us as workers emptied out of their office buildings. Soon, they'd be off doing much better things, filling themselves with happiness that most would never attain. That day, which had felt more like a month, came to a close before it had even begun—all without any farewell fanfare.

Miles of telegraph wire swung from pole to building like noodles of cooked spaghetti dangling between the fork and mouth. The Valley of Ashes made the rest of the city look pristine, but in reality, the whole city was one big wasteland, plagued by rapid industrialization that had swept the nation.

Although the sun had begun to set on the city, the summer heat still burned my skin, reminding me of its presence.

The people living in the Valley had become accustomed to higher temperatures, but that day was something else. The sun had launched a surprise attack at the weakest point. An unknown amount of casualties suffered. Of course, it was the hottest day of the year, and it seemed even more oppressive in the city—I had no clue how anyone could stand to be inside those stuffy buildings on such a day.

"Martin! Martin! Martin!" a familiar voice rang out behind me, waking me from my fever dream.

I spun around, almost tripping over my feet. In the distance, a man waved his arms like a maniac, jumping up and down as he came closer to me. His eyes, covered in streaks of cherry red lines, scanned me up and down.

"Carl?! What are you doing here?" I shouted as he came closer.

"I hopped on the next train after you left." He placed his hands on his knees and panted heavily. He let out two gigantic coughs before continuing. "I thought you were heading to the city to start the next phase or something—the backup plan. I get that you're upset about what happened to our stand, but I know you'll figure something else out. You always do. We just need to stay the course, that's all."

I was confused by Carl's overly optimistic and bubbly persona. Usually, he would have joined me in my despair, but this time, something was off about him, and I couldn't quite figure out what exactly had changed...

I didn't have the heart to tell him that there was no "next phase" to my plan—at least not yet. I had no backup plan, and I had no money. Every penny that I had to my name had been torn to shreds by that car.

As to staying the course, there was no course to stay on—two reckless road racers had obliterated the only course we could have followed.

Carl and I continued along the bustling streets as I contemplated how to tell Carl that the jig was up and that it would be best for him to return to the Valley and prepare for whatever job he still had.

A father and son shined the shoes of two Wall Street regulars. As we passed, the shoe shiners gave a friendly nod to Carl as he smiled and waved.

"You know them?" I asked, slightly confused by the interaction.

"They're some of my father's friends. They offered to let me work with them today, but I told them that I had already promised to help you first."

I looked down and sighed.

"Where are you going now?" Carl asked as he shuffled sideways, trying to keep up with me as I picked up my pace.

"I'm going to find Otto. I'm going to tell him what happened. Then, one of two things is going to happen. Either he's going to tell me to go work at the ash company like he did this morning, or he's going to help me take revenge for what happened to us."

"Revenge? What do we need revenge for? It's just a crate of oranges, Martin. We don't even know who did it. Why are you so worked up about a crate of oranges?"

"Just a crate? *Just a crate of oranges?* That was our future, Carl," I snapped, trembling as the disastrous scene replayed in my head.

"Martin, you didn't even pay for it. That old man paid for it—remember?"

A cool breeze hit me. I nodded as Carl yanked me back into reality. He was right. Revenge, at this point, was futile.

As we walked deeper into the heart of the city, construction workers dangled above us, laying bricks for half-completed office exteriors. One day, those buildings would blend right into the monochrome skyline.

"Now that looks fun, dangling up there like that," Carl said with a grin as he strained his head to look up at the workers.

If one slipped, they would plummet straight to their death, I thought.

"It looks fun because you've never done it before. Imagine doing that every day for ten hours. I'll bet it would get boring fast."

"I suppose it would. Wouldn't it?"

At that moment, I secretly hoped that Otto and I could escape the Valley and return to Germany, away from this sick, unforgiving country. I'd help him in tending to his family farm. Otto would milk the cows, rising early in the morning to care for them while I plowed the endless fields, planting whatever crop fetched us the most at the local market. He'd bring me to his childhood home and introduce me to the graves of his parents, who had stayed behind in Germany, never getting caught up in the lure of the American Dream; they were wise to avoid such a frivolous aim.

8

Chapter 8

Nestled between two otherwise normal-looking high rises stood a silent switchboard office abandoned by those who had once occupied it. Its boarded-up windows and burned brick facade differed greatly from Otto's vibrant description of the place.

In the past, a flurry of calls entered and exited the small office as they bounced back and forth all across the country. Never before was such instantaneous communication possible. Now, you could relay your hopes, dreams, and whatever else you fancied anywhere in the entire world. However, at that moment, a taste of what was and used to be but was no longer lingered in the stale air.

From the safety of the opposite side of the road, we watched batches of people scurry by, ignoring the strange structure, as they made their way through the waning City that prepared for the impending night. They were oblivious to the deviants that lived among them, operating in the shadows right beneath their very noses.

"Otto should be right in there," Carl said as he pointed to the dilapidated building.

I looked left and right before approaching the building. Except for a handful of stragglers, the roads had quickly emptied as most workers had already made their way to the nearest train station—or the nearest speakeasy.

We entered through a narrow gap in between the wooden boards covering the windows. The switchboard office sat empty and quiet, but a faint glow came from a door along the back wall. The sound of music seeped through the cracks, pulling us near.

I knocked on the door three times and then placed my ear on the door's cold, metal surface. I shivered. Rust rubbed onto my ear lobe and upper cheek, staining my ash-covered face a reddish brown.

From the other side of the towering door, a voice, stern yet calm, asked, "Password?"

I shrugged my shoulders and looked at Carl.

Carl cleared his throat and muttered, "Swordfish."

"What?"

While looking down at the ground, Carl spoke in a hushed tone, "The password is *swordfish*."

I calmly answered, "Swordfish."

My answer was first met with silence, but then the reinforced door clicked and swung open wide, revealing a bustling speakeasy filled to the brim with booze and bumbling fools.

A wave of music crashed over us, dragging us into the sea of speakeasy shenanigans. The brick walls, lined with shelves of every beverage imaginable, listened to the gossip that poured out from each patron.

Tucked along the wall opposite the bar, a band consisting of three middle-aged men played loudly while a woman crooned a sweet Jazz tune; her body swayed suggestively with the music. Her eyes danced between the patrons, flirting with them all as she sang.

The constant chattering of enigmatic creatures produced a deep hum that muffled the music and relegated it to the background. A few curious eyes darted up at Carl and me as we entered the room, but most people were too engrossed in their drink or hushed conversation to notice us. The energy had died long before we had arrived.

The music and voices created an incomprehensible slop of language:

"No, we absolutely won't be— How much? Yes, Mr. Köhl...I already met with Dr. Driv... Have you read that man Marx? Does she know yet—? Another drink, please.

My head snapped around as I thought I heard a familiar voice. However, I kept my hand on Carl's shoulder as he guided us through the crowded room. Avoiding the occasional glare from the wandering eye, we bowed our heads to maintain a level of disguise.

"Do you see Otto?" Carl asked, shooting his head left and right.

"No. Not yet. How about you?"

"Nope. Nothing. I don't see him anywhere," Carl said as he looked intently at each man's face.

A scrawny man slumped onto his table like a fishing hook. He buried his rosy face in his arms, hiding it from the crowd. Momentarily, he looked up, raised his glass, and took a swig of his drink before returning to his cocoon.

His glasses hugged his face a little too tightly. He pinched his nose, whisking away a patch of sweat.

I had seen those glasses many times before—it was Dr. T. J. Eckleburg in the flesh.

"Carl, look—look who it is," I whispered, grabbing Carl's arm and dragging him closer to me.

"What? That guy over there? Who is he?"

"You don't recognize him? He's on the billboard," I said.

"The billboard

"Yes, the billboard—the one in the Valley!"

"Oh—wow, yeah... you're right. That's him. They even got his glasses right."

The doctor's face, flushed from the many drinks he had downed that evening, rose once again from his folded arms. At least ten empty glasses sat in front of him.

His sullen eyes darted around the room, judging those who dined, following Carl and me as we continued our hunt for Otto.

An intricate platter, made a short time before the Civil War, rested on a shelf behind the bar. Below it, giant bottles of every type of bootlegged alcohol waited for indulgence. On top of the platter stood two porcelain figurines, each about the size of my fist. One, a young boy, and the other one, an equally young girl, faced each other, staring intensely into each other's eyes. A space no thicker than a piece of paper separated the two.

Their strange smiles suggested a never-ending entrapment in a complex state, somewhere between love and dissatisfaction. The girl wore a magnificent lavender dress and small, shiny white shoes. Two identical white bows tied in her brown hair perfectly completed her outfit.

The boy, dressed rather sharply for his age, lacked a level of sophistication that would have made him impeccable. His suit and combed hair would have given off an aura of sophistication if it wasn't for the fact that his suit was oversized and his hair shot up in a spike towards the back.

The two figures remained frozen in time. Had I gone up there and pushed them closer, they would have started to dance.

As my eyes remained locked on the figurines, I tripped over a stray chair and nearly toppled into a party of people.

"Are you a part-time or a full-time idiot?" a man asked as he took a sip of his bootlegged whiskey. He shook his head and smirked at the two girls wrapped around his arms. They giggled at his backhanded joke, slithering further up his arms like two snakes. They shook their heads at us with a devious, yet almost flirtatious, smile.

"Keep walking, Martin," Carl muttered to me, tightly grabbing hold of my arm as if I were the one who needed to be restrained in times like this. Carl kept his head down, concealing his face from the party. If it had been Carl who had been mocked, the man's head would have ended up on the other side of the City.

No. And then, he called me Old Sport—Yes. How much longer until—? It's so incredibly hot today, isn't it? I knew we should have gone to the parties when we had a chance.

"I still can't see him. He goes here every day after work," I insisted.

"Maybe he didn't feel like going into the City today. It is awfully hot in here," Carl said as he once again wiped the sweat off his forehead.

We found an empty table and sat down, suspending our search. A man at the table next to us carefully read the evening paper as he enjoyed a drink. The newspaper smelled of fresh ink, which occasionally caused his nose to wrinkle in disgust.

In the corner of the room, drops of water fell from the ceiling into a prepositioned metal bucket—each water drop harmonized with my tapping foot and the smooth jazz to create a melancholy symphony. Like a fly on the wall, I watched as each patron's veins swelled with liquor.

Carl ordered a cocktail with ice. I declined with a wave of my hand.

I looked at Carl and clarified, "Even before prohibition, my father never had a single glass of anything. My father was always worried that if he started drinking, he'd never be able to stop."

Carl rocked his head back and forth as he pondered what I had said.

"I suppose he had a point," Carl said with a smirk.

"Look at all of these people. Not a single one of them seems to care that they are so out of touch with reality.

They'll keep drinking until they black out. Then, they'll come back and do the same thing tomorrow and the day after that."

"Perhaps they're crazy," Carl suggested.

"No, not crazy." I cleared my throat and yawned. "My father used to say that everyone drank for their own reasons—often good reasons. He never judged those who partook in drinking, even in excess."

Some of the older men sat with women who were young enough to be their daughters. Most of them were drunk, and those who were only half intoxicated were close enough. When they opened their mouths, they practically screamed; they were so loud. The worst of jokes still somehow elicited a flood of shrieks and laughs that sounded like crying hyenas. The men and women drank not to make life more enjoyable but to make it more forgettable—that's what my father used to tell me.

A young man plopped himself down at our table; his hair flopped to the side like a sad Arctic seal. He gently rested his drink down in front of him and held his hand out for us to shake. His flush face flashed a painted-on smile, but he was not gone yet—at least not entirely. Neither of us shook his hand.

"What are you two boys doing in a place like this?" he asked as he withdrew his rejected hand.

"What are *you* doing talking to two boys that look like us?" Carl asked with a tinge of hostility.

The man leaned back in his chair. The chair's wooden legs creaked.

"Why, I don't judge people based on their appearances. I'm a—businessman, after all. I live out on West Egg. I'm not like those snobby old money men from East Egg." He paused and glanced around the room. "Those guys wouldn't give you a second of their time. I also happen to be an amateur sociologist. You see, I study the struggles of people like you two so that I can understand my struggles and the struggles of others better."

"Well, we're a little busy here if you couldn't tell," I said, turning my hand over, signaling to the man that he was nothing but an inconvenience. Carl and I couldn't have been less interested in talking with such an ignorant man.

"Oh—yes, why, of course. I'm sorry to bother you. I was just—I'll let you return to your conversation then. My apologies," the man said with a slight bow. He left us alone and departed for a table filled with men smoking cigars and laughing obnoxiously. When he walked, the man's left arm swayed while his right arm remained anchored at his hip, motionless.

I turned back to Carl and sneered, "Struggles? Out on West Egg? Are you kidding me? What struggles could they possibly have out there in their fantasy world?"

Carl finished the rest of his drink with a giant gulp.

"Remember, they're people too, Martin. They fight with their spouses, worry about the future of their children, and grieve those they love when they die. Sure, they might not have the *exact* same problems as us, but that doesn't mean that their lives are free from struggle. They suffer, too. They're just—better at hiding it. That's all."

"That's awfully profound coming from someone of your intelligence."

"You're not the only one who spends time talking to Old Joseph."

A woman behind us screamed.

Carl snapped his head around. I jumped up from my chair, knocking it to the ground.

Someone must have dropped a bottle, I figured. My eyes darted around the room as I tried to find the source of the commotion. Then, everyone behind us stood up from their seats and gasped. A few started running towards the door in a hurry.

Bang. Bang. Bang.

A group of men spilled out of the double doors of the backroom. They fell over each other as more and more men piled into the dining room, each one of them holding a pistol in their hands.

One man clutched his chest and fell to the floor of the speakeasy. Blood began to pool beneath him.

Bang. Bang. Pop. Bang. Bang. Bang.

I froze. Carl grabbed my arm and dragged me towards the door as gunshots rang out all around us. He reached into his overalls and revealed a pistol.

Bang. Bang.

More people ran for the exit.

Bang.

Others chose to take refuge underneath their tables.

Bang. Bang.

Bottles stacked behind the bar exploded as bullets lit up the bar, obliterating the shelves of booze.

Pop. Bang. Bang

A flood of alcohol rain downed onto the floor. Sunlight reached through the bullet holes scattered across the thin walls.

Bang. Bang.

Carl painstakingly dragged me through the way we had come in. One man followed us out of the front doors, hobbling while blood poured out of his right shoulder. As the men outside realized what was going on inside, each man drew a gun from their coat and fired at will, oblivious to the bystanders who walked by on that summer evening.

Bang. Pop. Pop. Pop. Pop.

A bullet ripped through one of the men's chest, shattering a window in a nearby clothing store. He fell to the ground; he was motionless, like a photograph.

Bang. Bang. Pop. Pop. Bang.

Carl and I dove behind a parked car as we watched the chaos unfold from under the car's body. Tires screeched as they pulled away from behind the building, speeding off into the City, never to be seen again.

Two men appeared around the building's corner, each carrying a submachine gun. They opened fire on the crowd of men and women.

Brat. Pop. Bang. Brat. Brat. Bang. Brat. Pop. Bang. Bang. Bang. Bang.

A few bullets cracked over our heads.

"I've been hit!" I shrieked.

Carl quickly patted my body and pushed me back to the ground, "No, you haven't. Stay down, or your head will explode."

Carl let off a series of shots without a desired target.

Bang. Brat. Pop. Pop. Pop. Pop. Pop.

Some of the men wielding pistols returned fire—as they also fired on one another.

The men's jaws clenched as they fired shot after shot. Their brass shells rained down to the ground and bounced off of their suits. All of them showed a total lack of, almost psychopathic, regard for human life—at that moment, they even neglected their own lives. The storm refused to let up.

Bang. Bang.

Bullets continued to spray out over our heads as both sides, if there were even two sides, emptied their magazines. Glass shattered all around us, raining down on our curled-up bodies.

Bang. Bang.

Carl pointed at an open alleyway a few yards away. The gunfire drowned out Carl's words.

Bang. Pop. Pop.

When there was a break in the hail of lead, we both took deep breaths and made a run for it. Our feet splashed through puddles of blood. A few lifeless bodies grabbed at our feet in an attempt to get us to join them in their eternal slumber.

Bang. Pop. Pop. Brat. Brat. Bang.

The sound of gunshots continued to echo as we ran as fast as we could down that alley. Eventually, we made it out onto another busy road. This one was free from rogue gunmen.

What felt like an hour had been only a few minutes at most—that's the truth. We looked each other over for bullet wounds, but we were both unscathed except for a few scratches caused by splinters of shattered window glass.

"That was a close one," Carl said, grinning.

"What are you smiling for? We almost died!"

"That's the most alive I've felt in months," Carl responded. He rubbed at a blister that had formed between his thumb and trigger finger.

Chapter 9

Carl shoved his hand deep into his pocket and pulled out a half-empty pack of cigarettes. Propping up a cigarette between his lips, he lit it with the lighter that his father had given him the first time they had smoked together. Perhaps he believed that a simple cigarette could whisk away all of his problems and worries—how foolish, yet understandably tempting.

"I just bought them yesterday at the drugstore. Do you want one?" Carl asked, shoving the pack in my face. The smell of sweet tobacco sure was tempting.

"No. I'm all set," I said, shaking my head and pushing the pack gently away from me.

"Are you sure?" Carl asked, once again, holding up the pack in front of me with a slight shake.

"Yes, I'm sure—I don't smoke."

He withdrew the pack politely with an almost embarrassed look on his face, but he knew that I didn't smoke—I had told him plenty of times before. He must have figured that it was improper of him to forgo asking me if I wanted one; he couldn't refuse the temptation to share. With him, there was a chance that I would abandon my abstinence, he probably thought.

For most of my early years in the Valley, I had managed to avoid—enigmatic people. However, I once met a man in Mario's Drugstore; he kept two packs of cigarettes with him at all times. In one pack, he kept his regular cigarettes that he smoked, while in the other, he kept a set laced with enough cyanide to kill a horse.

"Where you'd get the gun from?" I asked.

Nothing. Carl continued to enjoy his cigarette, ignoring my question.

After taking a long drag from his cigarette, Carl broke the silence. "Maybe we could find a payphone around here. I could call Penelope and see if she's able to come and help us."

A stream of smoke exited his mouth. He grinned.

"What's she going to do for us?" I asked, shaking my head at his sickening smile.

"I don't know—help us find Otto—or maybe track down that man from the Market this morning. Maybe she's seen him there before. Maybe she knows him."

"No, don't do that. She wouldn't be any help at this point. What we've gotten ourselves into—it's no place for Penelope. Don't call her."

"Embracing tradition, I see," Carl sneered.

"What do you mean?"

"You don't think women can handle what we've been through today—getting chased through the streets, dodging crazy drivers, and almost getting riddled with bullets in a speakeasy? Let me guess. You don't think *Penelope* could handle it all, do you?"

"No, it's just that—"

Carl, still full of adrenaline from the shootout, turned to me and said, "No, you're right. She couldn't. She'd fold so fast. She might act all high and mighty, like one of those suffragettes, but she's still stuck in the last century like the rest of them."

Carl continued, "Women are still trying to navigate their newfound freedoms, that's all. You would think now that women have achieved their liberation, they'd finally break away from all traditions, not just the ones they didn't like. I don't blame them. I'd be confused, too, if I were them."

"What? Now, what are *you* talking about?" I asked.

"Well—"

"Well, what?"

"So, we both know that she's one of those liberated women—the ones who have been championing the vote and the whole women's progress thing, right?" Carl said.

"Right—I guess. Sure. So, what? Why does it matter?"

"Well, she still expected me to act my part when it came time to court her. You know, I felt like I was still in the last century. Aren't we *all* supposed to be progressing? Why did I have to be the one to ask her out on a date? Why couldn't she have asked me? All of these women love freedom, but they don't want to lose their competitive advantage!"

"*Competitive advantage?* Are you trying to say you feel cheated somehow? Come on now, Carl. Don't be a fool. You know, you sound a lot like my father when he was still alive."

"Maybe he was right," Carl muttered under his breath.

"No, he wasn't right. He was far from right. He was stuck in the past…"

"Stuck in the past? The apple doesn't fall far from the tree, I guess," Carl said with a smile.

I ignored Carl's quip.

"However, you don't want to go into the future with my father's ideas about the world. Do you actually have a problem with Penelope holding onto some sort of tradition? She's not alone, you know?"

"Oh, of course, she isn't alone! Do you think any liberated woman would ever place that burden on herself? Of course not! She'd rather maintain the competitive advantage her ancestors have held for thousands of years! That's what I'm trying to say, Martin! Don't you understand?"

"Would you quit saying 'competitive advantage?' Oh no, you had to comply with a little bit of tradition. So, what, Carl? Penelope is yours now. Why complain about something that doesn't even matter anymore? Now you're the one stuck in the past! See?"

"Maybe you're right. Maybe it's alright to be stuck in the past sometimes."

"See! I know I'm right. Of course, being stuck in the past can good sometimes. Otto stays in the past all the time."

"Oh, really? Does he?"

"Yeah, he's practically never left it. He keeps a small wooden cigar box underneath his bed filled to the brim with the past."

"Filled with the past? How can you fill something with the past? What's in it?"

"Mostly, letters, and pictures, and some newspaper clippings—you know, the past."

"I see."

"He keeps some things in there for me, too—of my past. I wanted him to throw them out, but he keeps them anyway," I said as I stretched my arms up and yawned.

"Like what?" Carl asked, scratching his chin.

"Some newspaper clippings from when my mother died."

"Oh—why haven't you shown me them before?"

"I don't know, but I actually grabbed one from his room this morning. You know, she would have been proud of us. She would have known what to do after our stand got destroyed."

I pulled out a newspaper clipping, unfolded it, and handed it off to Carl.

Remnants of a subway's wooded frame clogged a dimly lit tunnel, mangled as if a bomb had gone off. A heap of splintered planks and glass shards littered the dark, moisture-laden tunnel. In reality, the train had jumped the rails as it traveled along a sharp curve under the streets of New York. Hidden from the bustling world above, my mother perished alone.

"Wow. That's awful. I can barely tell that it's a subway car," Carl said as he held the clipping close to his face, staring at it intensely.

"I know. I've looked at the clipping probably a thousand times."

"You don't talk about your parents much. I know they both died, but that's about all you've told me."

"I suppose I can tell you more, but it's rather sad. Are you sure you want to know the details?"

"Yes. Go on, I'm not a crybaby like you."

I brushed off his slight insult.

"Yeah, okay. Well, my mother's name was Peaches—Peaches Köhler. She was supposed to travel to the city to visit her sister for lunch. Her sister was a bit of a recluse; I never knew her much. She had won the lottery once and lived with her husband in a nice apartment—far away from her family scattered across the tri-state area."

"In the city?"

"Yes, somewhere in the city. My mother was headed to see her when her subway car derailed."

"Did they find out how it happened?"

"The guy driving the subway had never driven a train in his life. Not even once! You see, there was a strike going on, and they didn't want to upset any of the businessmen who relied on the subway. So, they got some guys who worked in the office to start driving the trains to keep them running as if the strike had never existed."

"Morons," Carl groaned.

"That's exactly what Otto said. Anyway, no one ever went to jail for either—not a single man. They all walked free, while my mother never got to return home to the Valley."

Carl stared off into the distance and sighed.

"Do you think about her a lot?" he asked.

I thought it over for a moment.

"Yes, I do—all the time, actually. I still remember her face, too. She had a rather youthful complexion despite her age. Her nose was like a kitten's; her lips were thin, about the size of my finger. Her hair was still long—she refused to give in to the newer short styles of the day. She was a reserved woman, and my father liked that and kept her that way."

"So, did you like her better than your father?"

"Definitely—without a doubt. When she was alive, she was my voice of reason. I rarely talked to my father, and he only spoke *to* me—never with me. While my father insisted on being a replica of the Victorian father he had growing up, my mother always talked to me as if she was one of my best friends, showing me love that had no bounds. She taught me how incredibly wonderful a woman could be. I'd do anything to bring her back."

A flock of birds flew overhead. They flapped their wings gently as they danced through the air. I pointed up at them.

"In her free time, she used to enjoy watching those birds. She knew more about them than anyone I've ever met. Now, whenever I see a bird, I think of my mother and think that she's watching me. It keeps me sane in this otherwise insane world."

"Anything to keep you sane, I guess. Alright, so what about your father? How'd he die then?" Carl asked.

"Ah, yes. Jager Köhler, my notoriously old-fashioned and pessimistic father. He didn't last a month without my mother."

"A month? Only a month?"

"Yes, a month. I remember them telling me that my father had died from a heart attack. Some said it was a broken heart, and that may have been true. However, it wasn't a broken heart from my mother dying. You see, my father had been a staunch opponent of women's suffrage, and shortly before he died, they ratified the 19th Amendment."

"The one that gave women the right to vote?"

"Yes, that one."

"You think your father died—from woman's suffrage? It had to be just a coincidence, right?" Carl asked.

"I'm not a doctor, Carl, but I think that's what killed him."

"I suppose, but—"

"There was also the high blood pressure, but I think it was the Amendment that broke his heart and killed him. It made enough sense to me at the time, so I just stuck with it."

"Incredible. Absolutely incredible." Carl shook his head. "Well, then, how's your sister doing these days?"

"She's doing alright—I suppose. After my father died, my sister left the Valley and moved down to New Jersey with her husband. He works in the office of a construction company that builds new homes down in Florida. She works for the US Radium Company making clocks and pocket watches."

"I remember my parents told me your sister cheated on her first husband," Carl said.

I shook my head.

"No. It's the other way around, actually. Your parents must have listened to just the rumors."

"Really? Those were all just rumors?"

"Yeah. My sister's first husband—or better, her first fiance, had gone on a trip to French Indochina shortly before their wedding. When he came back, he was engaged to a young French woman whose father worked in the imperial administration. I was too young and naive to understand the significance of the affair, but now I realize how much damage it did to my sister."

"So she's married now, though, right?" Carl said as he scratched his chin.

"Afterward, my sister became attracted to any man that the cat brought in, regardless of their temperament. Her current husband isn't a bad man or anything, but she chose him out of spite, not out of love."

"So, what were the rumors about then?"

"Well, like most scandals, it made the local paper, and everyone asked her what she had done for her fiance to run off all the way to Southeast Asia to find a new girl. They asked my sister questions as if she was somehow the villain of the story and not her disloyal fiance who traveled halfway across the world to find a new woman when one who loved him was sitting right in front of him."

"Crazy to think he'd just do that without talking to her first. Did he give any signs to her that he wasn't happy? Couldn't have just happened out of the blue, could it?"

"No clue. Even if he had, my sister…she's oblivious to the world playing out right before her eyes; you could snatch something from right under her nose, and she wouldn't notice it. She never realized that my father disapproved of her for accomplishing too little but because she had accomplished too much in life. He thought she had far exceeded the proper limits of what a woman should do."

"I'm confused. So, your father was upset that he had a successful daughter?"

"Yes, well—basically, yes, she incorrectly assumed that if she just kept working harder and harder, my father would have somehow turned into a progressive thinker, ready to welcome women's progress with open arms. I was ninety-nine percent sure that my father died because of women getting the right to vote—he was no progressive and was never going to become one. Not a chance in hell."

While I thought I was unique because my parents died young, my parents were only a drop in the bucket of demise. More than a hundred people died, including my mother, on that subway. When I went to visit the hospital to see my father, I walked past rooms of dead and almost dead patients suffering from every known illness and injury known to man.

I remember the moans, groans, and screams for help as their dreams came to a close. They hung from the edge of the cliff of life by the tips of their fingers. Slowly, someone stepped on their hands, causing them to fall into the abyss below. They weren't alone, though; everyone walked along the cliff of life, trying to avoid its edge as they went about their day.

Hospitals were a place that I tried to avoid. A car could run me over, and as long as I had the breath left in me to speak, I would tell the men to leave me there on the ground and have the doctors come to me. I was not going to the hospital to die like my father. I'd much rather die at home—even if it were in the Valley of Ashes.

Death had become the norm of the past few years, reaching out across the globe with savage arms. There were the people who died from the War, the people who died from the mysterious flu that followed the soldiers home, and those who didn't die in the War. People died because of the trains and the morons that shouldn't be driving trains. People just died and died and died—I just wanted to *live*.

I was surprised we even had enough people left to function, but somehow, the city hopped along, albeit on a wounded leg. We all felt a little closer to the cliff's edge as each day passed by in that decade.

Just the thought of staying in the city sent shivers down my spine and caused the hair to stand up on my arms and legs. I needed to escape the Valley of Ashes one day, but I had no plans of moving to the city. I wanted to get far away from New York. If it weren't impossible, I would have liked to move to the moon.

Kicking a rock out in front of me, I said to Carl, "Last week, Otto tried tricking me into crossing the Brooklyn Bridge into Manhattan with him."

"Why would he bother trying to trick you like that?"

"I don't know. He kept telling me he needed to walk a little further so that we could see the Statue of Liberty a little better. As we inched closer to the other side of the East River, I realized his trick. Otto told me that he had an important meeting to attend and wanted me to come."

"A meeting?"

"I had asked who we were meeting with, but he couldn't say. I asked what the meeting was about, but he couldn't say. I asked him where it was, but, you guessed it, he couldn't say."

"Strange."

"Very."

I turned to Carl and asked, "How much do you think it would cost to buy the whole city?"

"You mean like all the land? Buy everyone's place?"

"No, no. I mean, like—buy the keys to a city. What's a man got to do so that he has the unwavering support of the people? You think you could buy the hearts of everyone in a city?"

"And why would you even want to do that?"

"I don't know. I just thought about some of those guys that everyone seems to bow down to. How'd they do it? Did they pay everyone off? For example, if I had enough money to walk into that orphanage and give everyone enough food and clothing to last them a lifetime, or if I bought everyone in the Valley a new automobile, what would that do? Would they be indebted to me, never able to challenge me in the future? Why would they ever cut off the hand that feeds them?"

Carl rocked his head from side to side as he pondered my reasoning.

"I suppose you're right, but you're odd for thinking about things like that."

Twisted vines covered the orphanage like a suffocating wool blanket. Its small windows were latched shut and looked as though they had not been opened for years. No noise of happy children escaped from the building's thick brick walls. The worn front door barely clung to its hinges, waiting for the right opportunity to divorce the building after the slightest gust of wind.

"Staying there was the worst two weeks of my life. When Otto finally came to get me—I can't even describe how I felt to get out of there. It was amazing."

"Don't you hate living with Otto, though?"

"Sometimes, I do. I suppose it could be worse, though. I could be stuck here," I said as I shook my head at the dilapidated building, wishing that all of the children inside would meet their Otto someday.

10

Chapter 10

Smoke billowed from the five-story office building as if it were on fire. I thought perhaps someone had left a fireplace lit in one of the rooms, but on the hottest day of the summer, that made little sense—something else must have been burning.

I double-checked the business card the man had given me at the market—I had the correct address. I looked up and down the street to see if anyone was watching us.

"This has to be it," I said, looking up from the business card at Carl.

"I'll wait outside while you go in. If I hear you scream, I'll run in, alright?" Carl said as he assumed a defensive position outside of the door.

"Why would I scream?"

"What if that guy you were talking to was a vampire or something? Then you might scream," Carl laughed.

"Alright. Fine. You can wait out here if you want to, but if I die, it's your fault. You're supposed to be my muscle," I reminded him.

The door creaked as I pulled it open. A small lobby sat vacant inside. On the far end of the room, there was an elevator that gave off a faint glow. I stepped inside and was greeted by an elevator boy not much older than I was.

"Where to?" he said with a tired smile.

"Actually, I don't know where I'm going." I grabbed the business card out of my pocket and handed it to him. "I need to go here, wherever this is."

He quickly looked over the card and pressed a button. The elevator jolted as it traveled upwards.

"Floor three. Take a right. It should be the only room with a light still on. Everyone else has gone home for the day," the boy said as he pointed down the hallway.

"Thank you for the help," I said, but he had already slammed the door shut.

The floorboards under my feet were loose, and with each step, a haunting creek cried out from below me. Following the elevator boy's instructions, I found the only door with a light on inside. I opened the door and was hit by a familiar smell.

A map of Florida covered a wooden table in the center of the room. Several cities were circled with what seemed to be a red pen. A large painting of Comiskey Park hung high on the wall above an ashtray with still smoldering cigar butts. A haze of cigarette smoke hung in the air. I coughed.

I peered around the vacant room, searching for a sign of Mr. Wolfsheim. I was alone, I thought.

Then, I heard a sneeze.

My heart pounded as the sound of footsteps grew louder.

I reached for the doorknob, but before I could make my escape, a woman with little black eyes appeared from behind a row of metal filing cabinets, frightened by my sudden appearance. A lonely cigarette hung out of her mouth. It contemplated jumping from her lips to the ground. She stared at me without uttering a word.

On the far side of the room, a second door emitted a faint glow; the light was on inside and escaped ever so slightly. However, the lady stood between me and this door, and clearly, she was not interested in letting me through.

"I'm here to see Mr. Wolfsheim. I met him down at the Wallabout Market this morning. He gave me this card and told me I could find him at this address if I needed his help."

"Nobody's in," she said, returning to the filing cabinets without acknowledging me any further. After realizing that I wasn't going to take that as an answer, she continued, "Mr. Wolfsheim's gone to Chicago. He's gone. Nobody's in."

She was obviously lying to me; I could see it in the subtle movement of her eyes. She thought that she was slick, but she was not. I knew better.

I heard the crash of papers falling off a desk from behind the closed door and then a metal latch click. The sound of footsteps seeped through the floorboard below me. Then, the room went silent as the woman and I stared at each other in silence once again.

"Can you at least pass along a message to him? Let him know that I appreciated the oranges he bought me but that my business plan didn't work out. He mentioned to me that he might have a business—"

"This isn't really a place for a boy, you know," she said, cutting me off. She took a drag of her cigarette and released a puff of smoke. "Shouldn't you be in school or something? There are laws about that, you know."

Her backhanded question made my skin boil, and I realized that I was wasting my time talking to her.

I stormed out of the office and took the elevator down, oblivious to the fact that the elevator boy was nowhere to be found, and exited the building onto the street. The rush hour crush had waned and given way to a few stray people who continued to roam the streets. I looked left and right; however, Carl was nowhere to be found, and the day had begun to give way to the silent night.

Part Three

11

Chapter 11

Defeated souls seated in rows occupied each train car departing the city. Drops of sweat from the man sitting next to me landed on me as the train jolted over a bad section of track. After a drawn-out day of working, drinking—or both, the inhabitants of Long Island returned to the safety of their homes, but not before their unavoidable trek through the Valley of Ashes. It was an unfortunate but necessary evil.

As we passed by the mountains of ash, a few of the men and women plugged their noses while others covered their mouths with their handkerchiefs in an attempt to free themselves from the disgusting air. However, I had long become accustomed to the startling stench, and my lungs, having stopped caring a long time ago, ignored the assault.

As we slowly crept into the desolate station, I pushed my way through the sea of people, stepping on a dress shoe here and there. When I made it to the door, I took one last look back at the crush of passengers and hopped off the train.

Out of everyone in my train car, I was the only one who got off at the Valley of Ashes; the other passengers looked at me with shocked eyes, wondering why anyone would want to visit such a place, but of course, I wasn't visiting; unlike them, I lived there.

I trudged home to Otto's house that night, still damp and penniless. The sun had set gently into the Earth's horizon, retiring for the night as it prepared to illuminate the next grueling day. Everyone on Earth viewed the same sunset, yet oh, how that sun came down on some harder than others, burning them to a crisp and leaving them to crumble.

A slight breeze blew off the water, but it was strong enough to make me shiver and wish that I had brought a second layer with me. I should have known that the hot sun would have left us, leaving us with nothing but a chilly night.

Doctor T. J. Eckleburg's judgmental eyes, illuminated by the flickering moonlight, glared down at me like an angry ogre waiting to pick on its prey. I considered matching his gaze, but my attention was quickly diverted elsewhere.

A crowd, no larger than fifty people, stood in front of Otto's house like a pack of ghosts. Some of the crowd cried while some held those who wept. Their tears dropped to the ground, creating small brooks and streams that flowed down towards the Flushing River.

The river poured out into the Atlantic Ocean, carrying a polluted mix of ash and bodily fluids: blood, sweat, and tears. A whole sea of fish, tricked by the initial sweetness of the drink, died from the toxic brew, ingesting every last drop. Go fishing, and you might just get lucky enough to find one that managed to survive.

As I approached the swelling crowd, most of the adults, many of whom I had known for years, ignored me, perhaps because their tears blinded them.

Finally, a young man not much older than me noticed my worried eyes scanning the people up and down. His name was Chester, and he worked at Otto's favorite butcher shop.

"Hey, Martin. I've—we've been looking all over for you. Where have you been?" Chester asked as our gazes met.

"I've been busy…never mind. What's going on?" I asked.

"You know Myrtle, right? Otto's daughter?"

"Yes. Yes. I know her. Why?"

"Well, someone ran her over right in front of her husband's garage."

"What? Myrtle? When?"

"No more than an hour ago. The car didn't even stop; they just kept driving. And—you don't want to see the body. Blood doesn't bother me all that much, so I took a look already. She got chopped right down the middle." Chester cut through the empty air with his arm. "She looked just like the cows after I cut them up in the morning. What was she even doing running into the road like that? Such a stupid girl."

I gulped at his gruesome description and felt a slight pang of anger at his unnecessary quip about Myrtle. Then, my mind raced, each one thought battling for first place in my crowded mind. Wait, what if—it couldn't be. No way, I thought. That would be an extraordinary coincidence…but *what* if?

"Chester."

"Yes?" he said as he looked up at the moon above.

"Did they say what the car looked like by chance?"

"Some people saw the crash. I think they said the car was blue. No, yellow. Yes, yellow. That's it. I remember it now. Why do you ask?"

"That's the same guy that destroyed my orange stand earlier! If I could get out to Long Island and track that man down, I'd—" I stopped, remembering Otto's previous warnings. "Never mind. Where's Otto? I have to tell him—"

"You can't do that, Martin. Not now, at least."

"Why not?"

Chester paused, took a deep breath, and then said, "He jumped off the Brooklyn Bridge. They're still searching for his body, but some people saw him before he jumped. He was standing high on top of the railing. They tried to stop him, but he kept yelling, 'I'm going back to Germany!' and 'The American Dream is dead!' until he finally jumped over the edge. Now, I'd argue that the American Dream wasn't even alive in the first place..."

Chester continued, but I tuned him out as the rest of his words floated into oblivion.

My legs imploded as I dropped to the ground, gaining the attention of the adults standing around me. I never lost conciseness and looked up at the towering figures looking down on me. I thought about crying out for help but realized that my words would fall on deaf ears.

Instead, the ground held me, prohibiting me from moving any of my limbs. I tried not to cry, but the levees began to fail. Otto used to tell me that "real men don't cry." I never saw him cry, and I couldn't imagine him ever doing so.

That day, I suppose I wasn't real. I was merely a figment of the imagination that had latched onto the cranium in an attempt to avoid destruction.

As I sunk deeper into the ground, I stared up at the cloudless night sky; stars winked at me as tears rolled down my cheeks, watering the non-existent plants beside me. My body ached, and my eyes were heavy, fighting with me to be closed.

I was broke—and broken. I learned that one of the only people who still cared about me, even if it was fleeting at best, died without even saying goodbye to me first. Otto hadn't been the best person to learn—well, anything from, but sometimes, you need people in your life to show you how not to act; those people can be some of the most incredible role models you will ever have.

I wanted to lie down for a while. Actually, I wanted to lie down for a very long time. The Earth embraced me, wrapping itself around my arms and legs, granting my wish. I shivered.

12

Chapter 12

The old man in the moon, looking awfully tired and defeated, somehow managed to crack an empathetic smile as I sunk deeper into the ash below me, crying in periodic bursts. The crowd turned their attention away from me, forgetting I even existed as they mourned the death of their neighbor Otto. Numb to my pain, the people stepped on me as they returned to their shanties one by one.

At that moment, the moon and the Valley were indeed twins, separated at birth but born of the same vile concoction of dust and dirt. Usually, miles of space separated them, but on that night, they couldn't have been closer to each other.

As the crowd dwindled, some men in terrifyingly stiff suits and eye-concealing hats stopped and briefly watched Otto's empty house. They didn't shed a single tear and, instead, exchanged satisfied looks at one another. After nodding in agreement, they continued back towards the station, hopping on the soon-to-depart train. Perhaps they were detectives or owners of the ash company searching for their star employee.

My stomach roared at me like a lion that had failed to catch its prey. I had skipped breakfast and lunch, figuring I would have had dinner with Carl after a successful day. I hadn't even snacked on one of the oranges, refusing to cut profit in exchange for temporary satisfaction.

I tried to rise from the ground, but my body refused; my despair dragged me down as my eyes filled with a mix of tears and ash. After a few more tries, I finally managed to get back on my feet, stumbling a little bit as I brushed off my filthy overalls.

I tried to get closer to Otto's house, but the policemen stood guard like toy soldiers. They had no clue who I was, and Otto kept no record of my existence.

"Excuse me," I said, tapping the shoulder of one of the policemen.

He turned around and looked down at me and spoke, "Can I help you?"

"Yes...I live here. Can I go in?"

"You? Live *here*? No. No, Otto Schulze lives here." He held up a piece of paper, reading it over. "It says here he's the only occupant."

I had no way of proving to the policemen that I had lived there—at least, not without going inside. To them, I was a stranger.

My stomach growled again. A fresh-baked pie sat on the windowsill of Donna's floor-level apartment; her window was wide open. I crept over to the wall and stood on the tips of my toes. Without looking, I reached over the windowsill, expecting to grab a slice of pie. Instead, a hand grabbed my wrist.

My legs froze.

Ice filled my veins as my heart pumped blood ferociously throughout my frame. A gust of wind lifted me off my feet, and before I had a chance to wrangle free, the hand pulled me up through the window.

I landed face-first on the floor of Donna's kitchen. I tasted blood trickling out from a cut on my lip. I rolled over and looked up.

A policeman stood next to Donna, holding a notepad and a pen. Next to him stood a smaller policeman with his baton drawn, ready to strike me down if I tried to fight or flee.

Donna could have done the right thing and explained to the policemen my relationship with Otto, but instead, she stared at me as if I had committed some egregious act, smirking as the policemen waited to strike me down. She remained silent.

In her defense, she was probably mad at the world for reasons unbeknownst to me—no one ever bothered to ask her why. Her grand plan for revenge on Otto began with my incarceration, I thought. Like most people at some point in their lives, she had probably been chewed up and spit back out by the world and its cruel, never-understanding inhabitants. Ever since, she had declared war on her fellow man, vowing to ensure their eternal unhappiness.

"What do you think you're doing?" one of the policemen bellowed, grabbing the strap of my overalls with his meaty hands.

"I was just hungry—I was running a fruit stand, and then the ashes ate the fruit. The cars took all my money. I was going to help Carl move out to West Egg soon. I just had to sell a few more oranges. That's all. Trust me, I was making *so* much…"

"This kid's lost his mind," the policeman said as he looked up at his partner with amused eyes, shaking his egg-shaped head.

His partner let out a coarse chuckle and scolded, "You'll never get anywhere in life by living a life of crime, kid."

I squirmed as they grabbed me and yanked me to my feet like a stray dog getting snatched up by the dog catcher, waiting to be locked up in a cold, damp kennel. A layer of ash stained their uniforms; they must have been regulars in the Valley.

They loaded me into the back of a paddy wagon as a small crowd gathered to watch my demise. I could barely see my hand in the darkness. However, the moonlight provided the occasional flicker of light. A slight stench of mold and mildew hung in the air, irritating my nose with every heavy breath I took.

As my eyes adjusted to the darkness, I quickly realized that I wasn't alone in the paddy wagon. In the corner, a shadow-covered boy sat all bunched up, scowling at me as if he was ready to attack. He looked at me with murderous eyes.

Chapter 13

Carl leaned forward, cutting the distance between us drastically.

I knew Carl wouldn't hurt me, but my heart still pounded like a hammer hitting a stubborn nail. I waited for him to speak, but he sat silent and eyed me up and down.

He looked like a grizzly bear that had been confined to a narrow cage, ready to attack whatever prey crossed his path.

"Carl? What are you doing here?" I asked him like a mother questioning her young child after stealing a cookie straight from the jar.

"I could ask you the same thing," he said as his smile grew more prominent, exposing his teeth that extended high into his cheekbones. His nose exhaled short bursts of air that resembled a mix of a laugh and a snort, as if he was having trouble breathing.

"Are you alright, Carl?"

"Don't worry about me, Martin. I'm alright. I'm doing great," he said as he rocked back and forth gently.

"Are you sure you're alright? You don't seem alright. What happened to you?"

"Nothing—well...while you were up in the office trying to find that guy that gave you the business card, I met this guy named Meyer Wolfsheim. He must have rushed right by you—you didn't see him? He stumbled out of the front door, all worried like someone was chasing him. He was a strange guy and sort of intimidating, but he seemed to be put together. He saw me standing there and asked me if I needed a job. I was confused at first, but when he pulled out a stack of bills the size of a brick, I couldn't resist. Next thing you know, he told me that if any of those Irish guys ever tried to bother us again, I should show them who the boss of the Valley of Ashes is. He made me promise something, though..."

"What did you promise him?"

"Well...I promised him that he'd have exclusive—I shouldn't tell you what I promised him—not now at least, maybe down the road."

"Tell me. Tell me—*now*."

"I can't—Wolfsheim told me I could tell you with due time, as soon as you agreed to...never mind. If I told you now without telling you everything else, I'd have to..."

Carl dragged his fat finger across his throat.

I got the message loud and clear, but I was curious as to what Carl was talking about. What had he promised Wolfsheim? How desperate had Carl truly been? Had I failed him?

Blocking out the questions as they swirled around my head, I said, "So, that still doesn't explain how you wound up in here."

Carl continued, "You see, I snuck up on those Irish boys just like Wolfsheim had told me to. You know, those boys that had chased us this morning. I whipped out the pistol, and two shots later, they dropped straight to the ground." Carl shook his head but smiled. "It was like two trees being cut down by a lumberjack! I just kind of stood there all scared, though, instead of running away. I hadn't given any thought to what I planned on doing after shooting them, and before I knew it, I was tackled to the ground by some pretty angry men. I thought they were going to kill me—I really did, but as I looked up, I saw a few policemen running up to me. All I could do was laugh and smile as if they were tickling me. Those policemen saved me from the mob, but of course, they also arrested me. And now I'm here, but we'll be fine; don't you worry, Martin."

"Are those boys dead?"

"Dead? Absolutely! Not an ounce of life left in either of their bodies," Carl said with a smile.

His two rows of pearly white teeth showed before he opened his mouth wide to let out a cackle. With his whole body shaking, Carl chuckled as I stared at him, unsure if this had been the Carl I had gone to school with and subsequently enlisted to help me in my business venture.

Carl took his right hand and formed a gun with his index finger and thumb, aiming it into the darkness of the night and pretending to fire off two rounds in rapid succession.

He screamed, filling the voice of his two imaginary victims. I wanted to scream, too, but remained silent instead.

"Just like that, Martin. It was just like *that*. Two shots, and they were dead."

My eyes widened, and I shivered. I couldn't exactly run away from him, but my whole body wanted to get up out of there and run. I wanted to run away—far away.

"Oh, yeah. Also, if it makes you feel any better, Wolfsheim knew Otto. Actually, I guess I can tell you the whole truth, I suppose—Otto was one of Wolfsheim's associates. And when I say *associates*, I really mean—never mind, I don't want to upset you. Otto was the one who gave me the—"

"I don't understand. Why wouldn't he tell me?" I asked Carl, refusing to believe the new reality I had just been introduced to.

My head swirled like a whirlpool; my stomach churned as my mind raced through every past interaction I had ever had with Otto, attempting to identify any hints he may have given me.

Otto? Involved with a shady man like Mr. Wolfsheim? Impossible...or was it? My body was ready to collapse, but I caught myself as I started to lean forward.

Carl continued, "I knew something was up when everyone suddenly stopped treating me like garbage after I started hanging around with you and Otto. Have you ever thought of that, Martin? Have you? Also, have you never once wondered how Otto owned his place while all of the other workers in the Valley struggled to maintain even a dainty little shack? Sure, Otto's house was still in the Valley, but that's because he ran the place. He was the King, Martin. The King! He ran it all. *Everything*. It was all him the entire time. Don't you get it? He controlled the flow of alcohol between Long Island and the City!"

Carl launched into a coughing fit. His eyes stained a deep red, glowed in the occasional flash of moonlight.

He continued once again, "He even paid off the guys who are driving this paddy wagon right now. Can you believe it? But, Martin, don't worry! We're set for life. Here I was, all worried that I wouldn't be able to take care of Penelope and the baby. All we have to do is work for Wolfsheim. We're rich! Otto left us everything—every last penny. Wolfsheim showed me. You'll see. Oh, and wait until you hear about Albert's hold on Wallabout Market—he and Otto worked hand in hand."

I stared at him as I struggled to process the information he had dumped in my lap.

"You're *crazy*, Carl."

"No, I'm not! You have to trust me! You lived with the man. You had to know? No? Know? No, know?"

Carl started laughing again; his whole body rocked like a clock's pendulum, twitching as he breathed in and out.

Then I realized Carl was right. I had been oblivious to the fact that Otto and I lived a much different life than most people in the Valley of Ashes. Thinking about it in retrospect, Otto had never been worried about money, where his next meal would come from, or how he was going to afford to put me up in his house.

Otto had always commanded a large amount of respect for such a frail, aging man. Even Donna, after rejecting Otto's advances, still seemed to respect his authority. Only out of grace did he comply with her demands to desist, ignoring her inferior position within the hierarchy that Otto must have established. It all made sense to me now, but a part of me still found it hard to believe.

The paddy wagon bounced along the pot-hole-ridden boulevard as we traveled away from the Valley of Ashes. Carl, with both sets of his teeth and gums still visible, smiled as he looked out the window, casting a giant shadow over my body.

He let off a few more rounds from his hand pistol, striking targets he'd never have to come face-to-face with. They screamed—I have trouble forgetting those screams.

A small part of me still hoped that Carl was lying to me, but then a small panel slid open, revealing the back of the driver's head. A large scar ran across the back of his neck. It was hard to tell in the darkness, but he appeared to be in his thirties; something about him was strikingly familiar.

His rough but reassuring voice carried into the back of the paddy wagon, "How are you two holding up back there?"

I was unsure how to answer his question. This all but confirmed that Carl had been telling me the truth. I shivered.

The driver continued with a hint of impatience, "Wolfsheim told me to drop you two off wherever you tell me to. So, where do you want me to take you? This thing only has so much fuel."

I hesitated for a moment, still unsure how to answer. Carl remained in a trance-like state, rocking side to side while staring out the window at the moonlit city.

Was he going to drop us both off together? Was the driver insane? For all I knew, Carl was ready to kill me as soon as he had the opportunity to.

Then, it hit me. This was my chance. This was my chance to escape the Valley of Ashes for good.

Then, Carl cleared his throat and stammered, "Martin, I think we should go back to the Valley."

"What!? To the Valley? Are you crazy? Why would we do that? We could go anywhere! And you want to go back to the Valley?"

Carl stopped swaying as much and sat up straight while looking at me dead in the eyes, "Martin, next year, this time, I'm going to be a father. I got to go back and be with Penelope and the baby. And you don't get it! Wolfsheim told me we have to—"

I shook my head and snapped, "No. Forget about Penelope. You don't even love her like I do! She doesn't even—smarten up for once, Carl! We're not going back! No chance—*zero*."

Carl remained silent as he quivered and returned to his steady rocking, biting his fingernails. I shook my head at him, thinking how stupid Penelope was for choosing a dimwit like him. I was the King, and he was nothing but a fool in my eyes.

He had violated the terms of our settlement—he had stolen Penelope from me, knocked her up without more than five dollars to his name, and somehow expected me to come along with a magical plan to fix everything.

"You're a fool, Carl. That's what you are, a fool!"

"A fool? Maybe she wanted a fool. A fool's better than someone like you who's always overthinking things."

"No—No. No, No, No. Admit that you're not happy with her. You haven't said a single positive thing about her all day. Whenever I try to bring her up, you shut it down. Go on now, admit it."

"Fine. I'm—I'm not happy with Penelope. There, I said it," Carl said, avoiding eye contact with me.

"I knew it! And guess what! She doesn't even care about you, Carl! Guess where she is right now? She's out at a party in West Egg with some other guy! I saw her leaving on a train while we were selling oranges. She was headed straight for West Egg. 'Doesn't go to parties anymore.' Yeah right! She played you good—*so* good. You're such a fool!"

Carl's face shrunk as tiny droplets of tears formed in the corner of his eyes. He shook his head and once again started to rock.

After silencing Carl and mulling it over, I answered the driver, who remained unmoved by Carl and I's heated exchange, "I don't care where you take us. Just don't bring us back to the Valley. Don't listen to him," I said, pointing at Carl, "I'm the boss here. And he—"

"Hold on a minute. You're not the boss; Wolfsheim's the boss. Remember that," the driver said with a sarcastic snort, cutting me off from delivering a final blow to Carl's ego. He continued, "I'll bring you away from that rotten spot for now—but you'd be a fool to throw away all that Otto built for you in the Valley. But I'll get you out of the city if that's what you desire. Once I drop you off, Wolfsheim will be in touch about setting up shop. Until then, try not to get yourselves killed—you seem like you are able to get people on your bad side pretty easily."

"But—" I started to say.

Ignoring my protest, the driver continued, "You both need each other more than you realize. He might be crazy, but so are you. You both are equally crazy, but I think that's what Wolfsheim likes about you two, though. He always chooses the people who can do him the most good, and most of the time, he chooses the crazies, the ones who have nothing to lose—the ones who are chasing after some lofty dream that only he can make slightly more obtainable. You two are no different than his normal recruits."

I tried to interject once again, but the driver continued, "We've been watching you two all day. That boy has saved your life multiple times. Be thankful for God's little gifts. He saw that you needed him, so shut up, kid. Alright?"

With that, the driver slammed the small door shut, once again sealing himself off from us. The paddy wagon jolted forward as it accelerated, tossing Carl and me onto the damp wooden floor. Our eyes met as we searched for something, perhaps our friendship, that we once had but had lost in the blink of an eye.

Carl pulled out his pack of cigarettes, slid one into his mouth, and lit it with his trusty lighter. A single cigarette remained in the pack.

"Do you want one?" Carl asked as I watched embers rain down from his mouth.

"Sure," I said as I snatched the last one out of the pack.

I rested the cigarette gently between my chapped lips. Carl held out his lighter.

"No, let me do it," I said, ripping it from his hand.

"Fine. You do it," Carl sneered.

I lit my cigarette and took a drag, letting the corruption consume me.

Chapter 14

The mountains of ash shrunk as we drove further away from the Valley. Eventually, they disappeared altogether without even saying goodbye.

I couldn't help but feel a bit of homesickness, as if the Valley of Ashes was calling out my name, begging for me to return. It was a bittersweet departure, but as you know, it was only a temporary one. At this point, I really shouldn't tell you more, but I can't resist the temptation. It's too enticing.

Eventually, I returned to the Valley to assume the...business Otto had left me. He ran quite a diverse operation out of the Valley. Sure, he was a bootlegger, a scammer, and a racketeer...and, at times, a great deal more. However, I consider those labels awfully demeaning. I consider myself a businessman. The people have their demands and desires, and I work ruthlessly to meet them. Nothing more and nothing less than that, I promise you.

Naturally, I suppose that you still want to know more about Penelope. I fear I haven't done her justice in my brief telling of her story. In a world full of fools like Carl and I, she refused to become one. Simply put, our story together is nonexistent—perhaps both of you find great joy in that fact.

Your head would spin if you saw all of the fights Carl and I had over her. The American Dream: constantly fighting for and over things just out of our reach...

But then I met you, and every ounce of regret I had with Penelope evaporated before my eyes. I never loved Penelope, I promise. Now, Carl—well, I'd rather not talk about Carl with you—not now, at least. Of course, you know he recently won the Senate election, and we... never mind.

However, Penelope and Carl are far from the reason that I'm bitter—without them, I wouldn't be the man I am today. It's much more complicated than that, you see.

I am bitter for one simple reason. That stupid summer day, I escaped the Valley not through hard work, determination, or skill but rather by the sheer fact that my father had chosen to entrust my well-being with a sly German opportunist who secretly controlled a sliver of New York City while everyone else, oblivious to the world around them, steamrolled through their busy day, attempting to bend the inelastic world to fit their dreams.

The End

www.ingramcontent.com/pod-product-compliance
Lightning Source LLC
LaVergne TN
LVHW092050060526
838201LV00047B/1315